It was all Adam's fault that she had left home as she did. Now he was trying to make amends—but Micky was suspicious. What exactly did he want from her?

Books you will enjoy
by KATE WALKER

THE CHALK LINE

At seventeen years old and totally inexperienced, Rowena had had no idea how to cope with a sophisticate like Leo Vincent. He had used her and then callously abandoned her without, apparently, a second thought. Now, six years later, she should have been able to meet him on more equal terms. But could she?

GAME OF HAZARD

Every moment spent inside Erin's isolated cottage seemed to confirm the presence of an intruder, an alien in her previously secure world. Who was the mysterious stranger? And what did he want with her?

FIRST MAN

BY

KATE WALKER

MILLS & BOON LIMITED
15–16 BROOK'S MEWS
LONDON W1A 1DR

First published in Great Britain 1986
by Mills & Boon Limited

This edition 1986

ISBN 0 263 75436 7

Set in Monophoto Times 10 on 10½ pt.
01–0886 – 59509

Printed and bound in Great Britain by
Collins, Glasgow

For all the Currys

CHAPTER ONE

'MICHAELA!'

Amanda Dennison's voice carried clearly from where she stood at the foot of the stairs, and in the privacy of her bedroom Micky grimaced wryly at the sound. When her mother used her full name in that particular tone of voice it meant that all was not well in Mrs Dennison's scheme of things, and just lately it usually followed that Micky herself was the cause of her disquiet.

'Michaela!'

The voice sounded closer now, clearly her mother was coming upstairs. With a sigh of annoyance Micky closed her book and slid off the bed. Somehow her mother had the unfortunate knack of knowing exactly when she needed time to be by herself and she invariably chose just that moment to bring up something she considered important.

Unhappily Micky noted the tension already growing in the muscles at the back of her neck and shoulders; her mother always seemed to have this effect on her. No, not just her mother, her father too seemed like a stranger these days—when she saw him, which was rare enough. She felt as if she hardly knew her parents at all and there were days when she really believed she didn't even like them.

Not that that was unusual, she supposed. Most young people drifted away from their parents at some point; a 'rebellious' phase was fairly common when you were eighteen. Most of her friends had experienced something similar and seemed to take it in their stride. But Micky wasn't used to being at odds with her parents and with her father in particular. It was only in the last two years that everything had changed so dramatically, and just lately they had got so much worse. She sighed again despondently as the bedroom door swung open.

'So here you are. Didn't you hear me calling? What are you doing, hiding away up here?'

'I wasn't hiding!' Micky protested defensively, wincing at the realisation of just how antagonistic she sounded as she did all too often these days. Her mother's mouth tightened and immediately Micky felt contrite. 'I'm sorry,' she said hastily, making an effort to improve the atmosphere. 'What was it you wanted?'

'Just to check you had everything ready for tonight. You are wearing the pink dress, aren't you?'

Micky bit her tongue hard, trying to crush down the irritation that rose up in her. They had argued this out repeatedly and in the end Micky had given in, letting her mother win.

'Yes, Mother,' she said carefully. 'We agreed on that, remember?'

But the slight relaxation of her mother's expression was only temporary. A moment later a frown crossed her face.

'We'll have to do something with your hair. I do wish you hadn't had it cut!'

This time it was even harder to bite back an angry retort. She liked her hair short, infinitely preferred the spiky, layered cut to the unflattering long straight mane her mother had favoured which had swamped her fine-boned features and looked top-heavy on her delicately built frame. Micky's mouth twisted slightly as she recalled her mother's horror when she had returned home from the hairdressers with her soft honey-brown hair cropped into the boyishly short style. Mrs Dennison's image of feminine beauty was founded firmly on the idea of a chocolate-box prettiness that Micky knew she could never aspire to. Her small, narrow face with its high cheekbones and rather wide mouth could never be considered pretty but the new, short cut with a wispy fringe falling on to her forehead framed her features perfectly, emphasising the almost oriental slant to her almond-shaped blue eyes and giving her a gamine, elfin charm that was all her own.

'Don't!' Mrs Dennison's sharp voice broke in on Micky's thoughts, making Micky aware that, unconsciously, she had lifted her hand to her mouth, biting down hard on the nail of her index finger. Knowing how much her mother hated her habit of biting her nails, she brought her hand down in a rush.

'Sorry,' she muttered ruefully, surveying the ragged edge of the broken nail. 'I didn't think.'

With an impatient sigh her mother snatched up a nail-file from the dressing-table and thrust it at Micky, who obediently tried to smooth the damaged nail. Not that it did much good, she thought rebelliously, there was hardly any nail left to be repaired, and her untidy fingertips contrasted badly with her mother's own immaculately manicured hands.

She did try, she told herself defensively. In fact she had almost conquered the nervous habit—but that had been before she had overheard that incredible conversation between her mother and father. Her actions mirroring her thoughts, Micky filed savagely at the offending nail, causing her mother to exclaim in angry protest,

'That's enough! You'll have no nail left! Really, Micky, your hands are a disgrace!'

'I try!' Micky protested. 'But sometimes I just forget—I'm sorry,' she added conciliatingly, acknowledging privately that that was the third time she had apologised to her mother in the last ten minutes. Clearly it was one of those days—but then her mother was always impossible to please before a dinner party and tonight was not just another social occasion which was why Micky herself had to be present.

There had been plenty of other dinner parties in the last two years, plenty of business associates and clients to be entertained, but this one was different. Never before had her father insisted quite so forcefully that she attend, never had there been such an inordinate fuss over what she should wear, how she should look. In fact, on almost every other occasion she had managed to escape from such tedious events and go out with her own friends—and Zac.

A faint, wry smile touched Micky's lips as she recalled Zac's comments on the man who was dining with them tonight. His reaction when she had told him the things she had overheard had been unrepeatable. Not for the first time Micky wished she hadn't come home early that night, hadn't heard her parents talking.

'Well, I have some clear varnish that might help a little tonight,' Mrs Dennison was saying. 'And there's a lipstick somewhere that will match your dress exactly. You can borrow it.'

'Thanks.' Micky made herself say it and it came out ungraciously. Perhaps she wasn't really being fair, resenting her mother's offer in this way. Mrs Dennison was only trying to help, make her look her best, she should be grateful. But she didn't feel grateful. She felt manipulated, used, like some prize mare being groomed for a show—a brood-mare, she added bitterly, because she knew the hidden motives behind this unwelcome concern.

'What time is Mr Rochford coming?' she asked awkwardly.

'Eight, he said. We'll eat at half past—or perhaps nine would be better, half eight is a little early. Now you will try and talk to him, Micky. Don't just sit there in one of your silences for God's sake. You know how important this merger is to your father—and Dennison's.'

It's not a merger! Micky wanted to cry. It's a takeover pure and simple—or it will be if you and Dad get your way! But she swallowed down the impetuous words and forced herself to ask if there was any way she could help with the preparations, fully expecting her mother's immediate refusal.

'No, all you have to do is make yourself glamorous.' An anxious glance at her watch destroyed the impression of being totally in control that Amanda Dennison had wanted to give. 'Heavens, is that the time!'

She turned towards the door, still fussing, then hesitated as her eye fell on the book lying discarded on the bed. '*The Language of Flowers*?' she said, her voice rising on a note of curiosity. 'What on earth are you reading that for? It sounds deadly dull.'

'I find it fascinating.' Micky tried to suppress the instinctive sharpening of her voice but only half succeeded. Her mother shrugged faintly.

'I would have thought a nice novel . . .' Her voice trailed off, her mind moving back on to her main preoccupation. 'Well, don't drift off into one of your dreams and forget the time, will you? You should start getting ready soon—and don't forget the nail-varnish.'

Alone again, Micky wandered to the window to stare disconsolately out at the garden. In the dim light of a late October afternoon it looked drab and miserable, the glory of high summer long faded to a damp dreariness. The lawn was buried under a fall of leaves, their bright colours dulled by the rain. Micky sighed. Of all the seasons she liked autumn the least, hating the slow disintegration of all the beauty that had filled the spring and summer months. Winter at least had its own stark beauty and she liked to think of the seeds and bulbs lying under the snow as if sleeping, waiting for the first touch of the sun to bring them to life again.

Her eyes went once more to the scattered leaves. Tomorrow Arthur, the gardener, would rake them all up and pile them on the compost heap that stood discreetly at the very end of the garden, well hidden from the house. Really, it was surprising that in her concern to have everything perfect for tonight her mother hadn't instructed him to come in and deal with them today. A smile crossed Micky's face at the thought, but faded as swiftly as it had come when she remembered just why her mother was in such a panic about this particular dinner. Abruptly she swung away from the window.

'Oh, damn Adam Rochford! Damn him and his wretched company! Why couldn't he have stayed in America?'

Pushing her hands into the pockets of her jeans, Micky slumped back against the wall and surveyed her bedroom gloomily. It was a beautiful room, decorated in a delicate colour scheme of blue and white, and it boasted every luxury money could provide, she even had her own bathroom. But even after nearly two years she still didn't feel at ease in it; like the rest of the house it didn't seem like a home.

Was it really less than three years since her life had been turned upside down by the arrival of a solicitor's letter? Just a long, white envelope addressed to her father, but that small event had had repercussions that still made her mind reel with shock when she thought of them.

Determinedly dragging her thoughts away from the past, Micky picked up her book again. Her mother might have spent the entire morning at the hairdressers and the beauty parlour, but it was far too early for her to be thinking about getting ready and she had no intention of making any more effort than she absolutely had to for a man she had never met—and didn't particularly want to! For one thing, she doubted that it was possible for her to look 'glamorous' if she worked on her appearance from now till doomsday, and for another she was only too well aware of what lay behind her mother's insistence that she should look her best.

In exasperation Micky flung the book from her again. It was no good, her concentration had gone. If the truth was told, she was bored; bored with the way she lived, with not being able to *do* anything. On an impulse she pulled a jacket from her wardrobe. She felt restless and unsettled. Half an hour in the garden would calm her.

The chime of the grandfather clock in the hall sounded like a reproach in Micky's ears as she mounted the stairs much later. At the far end of the garden, behind the rose bushes, she had found a flower-bed that Arthur had uncharacteristically left neglected and had been unable to resist the temptation to settle down to weeding it. The half-hour had stretched to more than twice that time and only the descent of darkness had forced her indoors.

Hurriedly turning on taps to run her bath, Micky caught sight of her hands and grimaced wryly at the sight of soil embedded under the torn nails. It was no use even thinking about using her mother's varnish now, nothing could make these hands look ladylike and elegant, no matter how she tried—and she had *meant* to try, to go along with what her parents wanted, anything to try to improve relations between them!

It was as she was doggedly scrubbing the grime from her hands that a small ember of rebellion lit up in Micky's mind again, an ember that turned to a flame when she took the pink dress from the wardrobe. It was a pretty dress, very feminine and sweet with its white lace collar and cuffs, but it was a little-girl-dressed-up-for-dinner-with-the-grown-ups sort of dress, not *her* at all. Her mother had chosen it for her, bringing it home in triumph as a wonderful surprise, but one look at the delicate pink silk had told Micky that it had been chosen for the daughter Mrs Dennison wished she had, not the Micky who actually existed.

With an angry movement Micky pushed the dress back in the wardrobe, heedless of the way she crushed the flimsy fabric, and hunted for something she could feel more herself in. Her hand lingered on a grey sweatshirt dress, hardly her mother's idea of something 'glamorous', but inoffensive, then her eye caught the dress she had bought only the week before; and as it did so the conversation she had overheard sprang into her mind.

'You've told Micky I expect her to dine with us on Friday?' her father had said, and at her mother's murmured agreement had gone on, 'I particularly want her to meet Adam, and not just because of this merger. I hope that they——'

A sudden burst of noise from the television had drowned the rest of his words and it was a few minutes before Micky caught any more of the conversation.

'. . . and of course he's on his own now with both his father and mother gone and his sister dying so young. I thought that if he could meet Micky, talk to her, get to know her, then something might come of it.'

Micky couldn't catch her mother's low-voiced reply but she heard how her father continued and his words brought a cold dread creeping through her veins.

'Well, yes, he must be thinking of getting married. He'll want children to carry on the business, and he'd have a lot to offer a wife. Think of the life she'd have, she'd want for nothing. But of course the girl Adam marries will have to have something to offer too. As the wife of such an important man she'd have to be above reproach, there'd need to be no suspicion that she married him simply for his money, so it would help if she had some of her own as Micky will——'

Unable to believe what she was hearing, Micky stared dazedly at the door before her. Was it possible? Was she being unduly sensitive or did her father's words imply that he had hopes of far more than a business connection with Adam Rochford? Realising she had missed the end of her father's sentence, she listened again and her mother's words deepened her worst fears.

'And if this merger goes through you and Adam Rochford will be partners. What better way to seal that partnership than to——'

Micky had interrupted the conversation at that point, pushing open the door and marching into the room. Her mother's uneasy start, the vaguely guilty look on her face, and the way she had immediately switched the conversation on to another topic left Micky in no doubt that the idea of a match between herself and the owner of Rochford Electronics was firmly fixed in Mrs Dennison's mind, a belief that had been reinforced by the worse-than-usual fuss her mother had made over this particular dinner party and her daughter's appearance at it.

Well, she would fool that little plan, Micky resolved firmly, pulling the new dress from the rail. She didn't want to be married—and certainly not to Adam Rochford! Her father's world seemed to centre around money, profit and loss (preferably the former) in a way it had never done before and she could well believe that the possibility of acquiring such a powerfully influential and wealthy son-in-law as Adam Rochford would be almost irresistible to him. She wasn't going to be a pawn in that particular game!

Micky shook her head slowly. It still didn't seem possible that her father actually *owned* Dennison's, that because of some clause in a distant and never-seen cousin's will he had left his modest position as a self-employed electrician and moved into the executive bracket. It was through Dennison's that they had come up against the Rochfords in the person of John Rochford, this Adam's father. That first important contract he had given Dennison's had been a lifeline to the smaller company which had been going through a rather sticky patch and since then her father had never looked back. John Rochford had put more and more work his way, profits had soared and continued to do so, and from that point Micky's life had changed dramatically and, in her opinion, very much for the worse.

They had moved from their shabby suburban semi to this large, elegant house, leaving all the old familiar things behind them. At fifteen Micky had felt as if she had been torn up by the roots and transplanted into a world she didn't know or understand, a feeling that had been intensified when she had been taken out of the local comprehensive and pushed into an exclusive, fee-paying all-girls school where she had floundered like a fish out of water. Her parents had told her she would soon make new friends—but how could you befriend girls who laughed at your accent, your clothes, your lack of sophistication?

She had grown to hate the name of Rochford, seeing all the changes that had taken place as a direct result of her father's connection with the giant corporation; even the hated school had been chosen on John Rochford's recommendation because he had sent his own daughter there. She hated the way her father changed, devoting all his time to his work, glorying in profit figures as he had once gloried in much simpler things like a spring morning or a day by the sea, things he no longer had time for. Her mother too had been swallowed up in the new life, obsessed with appearances and trying to force new ways of behaviour on Micky herself, determined that her daughter should behave like a lady so as not to let her down in front of her new-found friends.

Then John Rochford had died and his son had come back from America where he had been a director of a branch of his father's company to take over the whole operation, and like the proverbial new broom he was implementing major changes, not the least of which was the proposed merger. Adam Rochford was going places and taking Dennison's with him, her father had said, his eyes lighting up at the prospect.

Micky's grip tightened on the coat-hanger as her resolve hardened. She wasn't going to be part of the deal, a 'perk' of the merger between the two firms, married off to some boring old stuffed shirt more than twice her age! Old Mr Rochford had been nearly seventy when he died, so his son must be the same age as her father—and that being so, she knew exactly how to put him off and ruin her mother's matchmaking plans once and for all!

Almost an hour later, Micky surveyed her appearance in the mirror with a sort of appalled satisfaction. She and her mother had never seen eye to eye on the matter of clothes and the more Mrs Dennison protested at what she wore, the more some perverse imp of mischief urged her daughter to choose increasingly outrageous outfits. This time she had surpassed herself.

She had originally bought the new dress to wear to a discothèque and there it would hardly have merited a second glance, but in the conventionally elegant surroundings of her parents' home it looked wild to say the least. The soft material, a mock leopard-skin print, clung provocatively to the slim lines of her body, emphasising her almost boyish slenderness. It might have looked better if she had had a few more curves, Micky thought, having always considered her slight frame too thin and childlike to be even remotely feminine, but she had done her best, cinching in the dress tightly around her tiny waist with a wide belt which had the effect of pulling the already short skirt up even higher, revealing an amazing extent of her long slim legs. She had chosen black fishnet tights and the highest-heeled pair of shoes she possessed, feeling the need of a few extra inches to give her more confidence. One of the disadvantages of being so small was that it was almost impossible to look any man straight in the eye—and she was determined to do just that with Adam Rochford, she wanted to see his reaction to everything she said or did.

The sleeveless, vest-shaped top of the dress revealed every inch of delicate arms that seemed almost too fragile to bear the weight of the heavy silver bracelet she wore and she had filled in the low, scooped neckline with rows and rows of chains. She had gone to town on her make-up too, exaggerating the slant of her smoky blue eyes with black kohl and blending silver and blue eyeshadow until the effect was reminiscent of that found on the masks of the Pharaohs.

On a final crazy impulse Micky reached for a can of spray tint that she had been urged to buy by Susie but had never had the nerve to try before and added bright blonde streaks lavishly over her own silky brown hair.

There! she told her reflection defiantly. That should do it! Her appearance would probably send her father's blood-pressure soaring and reduce her mother to a state of horrified hysteria, but if Adam Rochford was anything like the other pompous, middle-aged, stick-in-the-mud old fogies she had met at the few dinners she had been coerced into attending he would *never* consider her a possible candidate for the role of Mrs Rochford, his consort and mother to a dynasty of next-generation Rochfords now—which was just the way she wanted it. Hastily she left her room before her nerve failed her at the last minute.

The clock was striking eight as Micky descended the staircase. She had timed it just right. The great man was due at any minute so even if her parents saw her before he actually arrived there would be no time for them to force her to go and change without causing a delay and the sort of upset her mother would sell her soul to avoid. Micky almost ran the last few steps across the hall in her haste to get the inevitable confrontation over as soon as possible.

The drawing-room door stood ajar and she pushed it open and moved into the room, her head held high, then stopped dead in astonishment, a small gasp of shock escaping her lips as she registered the fact that her parents had not come down yet and the room was unoccupied—except for the man standing by the window.

He had his back to her and was apparently absorbed in studying the titles of the books on the shelf before him, not having heard her come in, so she had a few seconds' grace to study him and decide just what her next move would be.

Not that what she could see gave her much to go on.

Her main impression was of a long, straight back held firmly erect and topped with a pair of broad shoulders around which a superbly tailored charcoal-grey suit fitted snugly. *Not* a dinner jacket, Micky noted automatically. Her mother would be disappointed about that, but no doubt Dad would be relieved. He had come a long way from the man who had had to be forced into a suit for a family wedding or the like but he still wore his expensive clothes with a faint unease, unlike this man who, even from the back, looked as if he put on a two-hundred-pound-plus suit as casually as Zac wore his ancient, battered leather jacket.

He looked tall, but then to her five feet two inches almost every man gave that impression, and his hair was a rich chestnut brown with a faint glint of copper in its thickness. Micky had barely time to reflect that it was more stylishly cut and worn rather longer than she would have expected in a man in his mid-forties before the door banged shut behind her and, alerted by the sound, Adam Rochford swung round to face her.

Without thinking, Micky took an involuntary step backwards, unnerved at the prospect of finally coming face to face with the sole surviving member of the family whose influence had so devastated her peaceful existence. Confused impressions of a lean, strong-boned face, strange-coloured eyes of the sort that could be light brown or green depending on the light, and a firm, determined jaw bombarded her, but the most bewildering thing of all was the realisation that her assumption about his age had been way off the mark. This man was not in her father's generation at all!

Then her mind cleared, her resolve hardening as it did so. He was still *years* older than she was, far too many for her to want to be trapped into marrying him. She saw those hazel eyes widen slightly in surprise and could almost have sworn that a glint of amusement, hastily suppressed, appeared in them briefly. The suspicion made her prickle with irritation. She didn't know if he was party to her parents' scheme to marry the two of them off, and didn't care. Her head came up defiantly and she met those light eyes with undisguised hostility as the man took a step towards her.

'You must be Michaela,' he said smoothly and his low-toned voice held just a hint of an accent that was the result of his years in America and which, infuriatingly, because she didn't want to like anything about him, Micky found disconcertingly attractive.

Automatically she nodded a response to his implied question, the movement brusque and unfriendly. She didn't like the way he looked her up and down, all amusement gone, replaced by an impassive and deliberate survey of her appearance. The coolly assessing gaze angered her, she felt like a specimen under a microscope and without that touch of amusement his eyes were cold and distant and not at all friendly. Resolutely she stared back, her chin lifting slightly. Too late she realised that he had held out his hand in greeting and, unknowingly, she had ignored it. Now he let it drop back at his side, his mouth twisting slightly almost as if he had expected just such a reaction.

'Bill's told me a lot about you,' Adam Rochford commented disconcertingly, making Micky long to know just what her father had said. *Had* her mother's suggestion of a marriage taken root in his mind so that he had told this man about her in the hope of arousing his interest, and, worse still, had Adam Rochford considered the idea of such a marriage himself, attracted by the lure of one day owning both companies? The thought jolted her into speech at last, her words coming out in a taut, uneven voice.

'And you're the notorious Mr Rochford, I suppose.'

The firm line of Adam Rochford's mouth twitched very faintly at the corners but his voice was distinctly cold as he said, 'Adam, please—and I hope notorious is just a turn of phrase. I had no idea I had such a reputation.'

'What I mean is I've heard nothing but your name and what you've been doing for—oh, six months or more now,' Micky returned tartly. 'We've had Adam Rochford at breakfast, at dinner, and even all through Sunday lunch. After all I've heard I'm surprised to find you're just a human being. I'd expected Superman at least.'

The words were out before she had time to consider how appallingly rude they sounded. They weren't exactly true either. Her father had been full of admiration for Rochford Electronics' new managing director and had praised his business acumen certainly, but in no way had he idolised the other man as she had implied, and really it was Micky's own uneasy feelings about her parents' motives that had made her feel that there had been no other topic of conversation than Adam Rochford in recent weeks.

'I am quite human, I assure you,' Adam said and something undefinable in his voice made Micky's stomach twist nervously. It wasn't what he had said but a slight, hard undertone to that low, attractive voice that told her that Adam Rochford was not a man one tangled with lightly. She felt reproved, like a child caught showing off, and the feeling was not a comfortable one. It made her jittery, her eyes sliding away from his as she hunted for something to say. She had never been very good at making polite conversation with her father's business associates and the matter was complicated by this man being not at all what she had expected.

It was in this awkward moment that she noticed the flowers, a huge, cellophane-wrapped bouquet lying on the coffee table, and with an instinctive cry of delight she crossed the room for a closer look.

'These are beautiful! Are they for Mother?'

Adam inclined his head slightly in agreement, the offhand gesture seeming to imply indifference to the magnificent bouquet. Probably he had simply instructed his secretary or some other member of his staff to order them for him, Micky thought irritatedly. No personal effort had gone into his gift. At this time of year such flowers must have cost a fortune but the money didn't mean a thing. The bouquet was just a gesture, a lavish, extravagant gesture to be sure, but one with no feeling behind it. It meant nothing.

Suddenly reminded of the book she had been reading, Micky studied the flowers more closely. Roses of course, red and white, carnations—heavens, even orchids! Urged on by an imp of mischief, she spoke her thoughts out loud, assuming a deliberately satirical tone.

'You are beautiful. I offer my love and devotion. Alas for my poor heart! I am worthy of you.'

Micky slanted a teasing glance at Adam's face. If he was bewildered he hid it well, only a faint narrowing of his eyes betrayed any response.

'Is that what you wanted to say to my mother?' she asked archly, then went on hurriedly, her voice sharpening in unease at the way he made no response but calmly continued to study her without a hint of expression on his face. 'Because that's what your flowers say. Orchids—you are beautiful—red roses, love and devotion, and the white ones mean I'm worthy of you . . .'

Her voice faltered on the last few words. She wished she had never started the joke now, it had fallen very flat indeed, and that steady, assessing gaze was distinctly unnerving.

'I had thought of buying flowers for you too.' Adam spoke at last, his tone dry and ironical. 'But perhaps it's just as well I didn't; you might have read more into them than I intended.'

Deep inside, Micky felt a small pang of regret. No man had ever brought her flowers, the boys of her own age never considered such thngs important. She touched the flowers lightly, regretfully, and then wished she hadn't for she knew the slight gesture hadn't been missed by those sharp, probing eyes and it didn't fit with the girl she wanted him to believe her to be.

'I'm glad you didn't. I don't go for that sort of meaningless gesture—you'd have wasted your money.'

'So it seems,' was the softly spoken response and once again Micky sensed that hard undertone to his voice. She was sure that Adam was about to say something more but at that moment the door opened and her father strode into the room.

'Sorry to keep you, Adam. I hope you haven't been too bored.'

'Not at all,' Adam returned smoothly. 'Miss Dennison has been—entertaining me.'

That brought Bill Dennison's eyes round to his daughter. Micky saw him blink hard, the smile that had hovered on his mouth fading rapidly to be replaced by a red flush of anger as he took in her appearance. Micky met his eyes defiantly.

'Hi, Daddy!' she declared with all the brightness she could muster and was suddenly intensely grateful for Adam's presence in the room, because it forced her father to swallow down the anger he was feeling, unable to express it in anything beyond the furious glare he directed at her before he turned his attention back to his guest.

Drinks were poured, Mr Dennison pouring Micky a sherry automatically and then ignoring her completely, and she was glad to subside into a chair and sit quietly, needing time to think. When she had started on this little farce she had had only one thought in her head—to show Adam Rochford that he and she were worlds and generations apart and so ensure that the idea of a merger with the Dennison family as well as the company never entered his head—and, once having started, there was no going back, but she had never really considered how she would cope with her father's anger, an anger that she knew only too well was carefully concealed under his polite conversation with his guest and which marked yet another stage in the disintegration of their formerly loving relationship. The curse of the Rochfords had struck again, she thought with bitter flippancy. Once again the interference of one of that family in her life had resulted in disaster.

Micky's eyes slid to Adam's face, watching him covertly. Quite human, he had said, and he certainly looked human enough now, relaxed and at ease, lounging back in his chair, chatting to her father with an easy friendliness. But those brief moments when she had seen that underlying hardness in him made her doubt that the description quite fitted. He was really quite good-looking if you liked the sleek, expensive type—not her sort of man, of course, he was much too smooth for her taste. Few of her friends possessed any clothes beyond the usual jumper and jeans and she could just imagine Zac's reaction to that suit.

Zac. Resentment flared again making Micky shift restlessly in her seat. If it hadn't been for this wretched dinner party she would have been out with Zac now, among her own friends where she felt relaxed and free to be herself, which was not at all how she felt now.

She glanced at Adam again, her mouth twisting as she saw him smile at something her father had said. He looked completely at home, she thought angrily, a welcome guest while Zac was openly disapproved of, his visits actively discouraged by her parents. A few years ago they wouldn't have minded him at all, she told herself bitterly, but now he just wasn't good enough for the daughter of the owner of Dennison's.

They had met at a dance to which Micky had gone with Susie. With his jet-black curls and blue, blue eyes and the sort of brooding sexuality of a young Marlon Brando, Zac had been the centre of a great deal of feminine attention but it was Micky he had singled out from the crowd, Micky he had been seeing ever since. From the start he had swept her off her feet and she hadn't touched the ground since. Live for today and let tomorrow go hang was Zac's philosophy, an attitude so much in contrast with the inhibited, restrictive obsession with appearances that was her home life that it had acted on her like a draught of strong wine, liberating and exhilarating her so that she had fought her parents' opposition as fiercely as a tiger defending her young, but to no avail.

From under her lashes Micky glared at Adam Rochford. This was the man her mother and father had set their sights on as a son-in-law, this sleek, cold-eyed creature who exuded such an aura of wealth and self-assurance. It was there in every movement, every gesture, in every inch of that elegantly suited frame. Well, his clothes might impress her parents but they did nothing for Micky herself. She had seen more than enough of such suits on her father's business colleagues to realise that an expensive exterior often hid a decidedly dull and boring interior and she rejected everything Adam stood for—the materialistic approach to life that put the acquisition of profit before other, more human concerns.

'Michaela, what *are* you wearing!' Amanda Dennison's voice broke in on Micky's thoughts. Absorbed in her reverie she hadn't noticed the door open again but now she lifted her head with a start to meet her mother's eyes.

Mrs Dennison had none of her husband's ability to cover up his feelings. She gazed at Micky speechlessly, her eyes wide in a face that was pale with shock and anger. Belatedly Micky recalled her earlier resolve to try to improve relations between herself and her parents, a resolve forgotten in her determination to prove to Adam Rochford that she was not his type at all. Half of her wanted to say she was sorry, it was all a joke, and offer to change at once but the other half of her mind rebelled violently. She was not a child any more! She would wear what she liked.

'Amanda——' her father began but Micky cut in on him.

'It's just a dress,' she said defiantly, the tangle of feelings inside her made ever worse by the way Adam Rochford's eyes had swung to her face watching every fleeting expression that crossed it.

'A dress!' her mother exclaimed. 'I would hardly call it that! It looks more like something from a rag-bag to me!'

'I think that's the idea,' a quiet, softly accented voice put in. 'I believe it's the fashion to look as if you found your clothes in a dustbin.'

Adam had risen to his feet at Mrs Dennison's entry and now, having drawn her attention to himself, he crossed the room towards her, his hand outstretched in greeting.

'I'm delighted to meet you at last, Mrs Dennison,' he went on urbanely. 'I'm sorry it's taken so long, but I've been sorting out my father's affairs and of course I've only been back in England permanently since August.'

As Micky watched, her mother's anger ebbed, giving way to an ambarrassed confusion as she took the hand Adam held out to her and murmured an incoherent greeting, evidently torn between her earlier feelings and her abhorrence of any sort of scene in front of a guest. She even managed a shaky smile in reply to Adam's compliment on her appearance and within a few minutes was answering his polite questions about the house in a much more relaxed manner.

Very clever! Micky thought, admitting to a grudging admiration for the way Adam had defused a potentially explosive situation, but an admiration mixed with resentment at the way he had moved in and taken over as if he had every right to interfere. Who did he think he was? She was perfectly capable of standing up for herself without his help!

He had presented the bouquet now, brushing aside

her mother's flushed gratitude with a practised ease.

'I'm glad you like them. I always like to bring flowers for the *lady* of the house.'

The faint emphasis on the word and the mocking glance he shot in Micky's direction had her sitting stiffly erect, her skin prickling with irritation.

'Personally I think it's a wicked waste to cut flowers,' she said sharply. 'It's like killing them.'

'But in this weather they'd die in a day or two anyway,' Adam countered quietly. 'You have to agree they'll last much longer indoors.'

The words were spoken blandly but there was a definite challenge in the light eyes, a challenge Micky was unable to let pass.

'Flowers look much more beautiful left growing naturally,' she declared, and saw one eyebrow lift in sardonic questioning.

'You surprise me,' Adam drawled silkily. 'I thought beauty and anything natural was distinctly passé these days. The current craze seems to be to make everything as ugly as possible.'

Hazel eyes locked with blue before Adam let his gaze slide down over her body taking in the offending dress, lingering briefly on the length of slender, black-covered leg exposed by the short skirt before flicking back up to her face. Adam's faint, dismissive shrug seemed to imply the comment 'Case proved', and Micky felt hot colour burn in her cheeks as her temper flared.

'Not ugly, Mr Rochford, just different. I don't subscribe to the belief that women should dress just to please men.'

'Evidently,' was the murmured response. 'So tell me, why *do* you dress like that?'

'Because I like it!'

Once more a lifted eyebrow implied disbelief so that she blundered on thoughtlessly.

'I dress to express my personality. I wear what *I* like, not what convention dictates a woman should wear.'

Bill Dennison made a move as if to speak, but Adam was there before him.

'And how do your friends dress?'

'Like me, of course.'

'Exactly.' There was a note of satisfaction in Adam's voice making her wonder just what trap she'd fallen into. 'I'm afraid you're not as individual as you think, Miss Dennison. You just dress in a way that makes you acceptable to the group you want to belong to. In your own way you're every bit as conventional as everyone else.'

Micky opened her mouth to snap back an angry retort but suddenly found she had no answer at all and closed it again hurriedly, as a vivid memory of the day she had bought the dress filled her mind. She had originally been tempted by a more restrained style but had been dissuaded by Susie's scorn and her blunt declaration that 'Nobody wears that sort of thing any more'. It had been Susie who had picked out the leopard-skin dress, declaring that Zac would flip when he saw her in it, she just had to buy it, and Micky had succumbed to her persuasion.

At that moment she caught Adam Rochford's eye. Damn the man! she thought furiously, seeing once more that gleam of amusement she had detected earlier. He'd got her cornered and he knew it. Luckily the sound of the gong indicated that dinner was ready and so forestalled any further discussion.

To Micky's surprise Adam offered her a hand to help her up from her seat, a hand she could not refuse without being openly rude. His grip was warm and firm, the strength of his arm pulling her unnervingly close to the elegantly suited body so that she caught an intriguing waft of some subtle after-shave as she wavered for a moment, unsteady on her ridiculously high heels. Adam's hands closed over her arms to steady her and in the brief moment that he held her he bent his head and whispered in her ear, so softly that her parents heard nothing of what he said.

'One other thing,' he murmured, his breath warm on her skin. 'If that appalling outfit is meant to disguise the fact that you're female, it's only fair to tell you that it hasn't succeeded.'

Then as Micky gaped bemusedly, unable to believe what she had heard, he released her abruptly and moved to her mother's side, offering his arm, to escort her in to dinner.

CHAPTER TWO

IF there was such a thing as an ordeal by food, Micky thought wretchedly, then this was surely it. The meal in front of her was particularly appetising, Mrs Williams, the cook, had excelled herself, but Micky's normally healthy appetite had completely deserted her and she pushed the food round on her plate with a singular lack of enthusiasm. Catching her father's eye and seeing the reproving glare he directed at her, she speared a piece of chicken on her fork and carried it to her mouth but the effort of chewing and swallowing was almost beyond her.

She knew what that glare meant, she couldn't possibly have any doubts after the way her father had caught her arm on the way out of the drawing-room, holding her back until her mother and Adam were well out of earshot before expressing his opinion of her appearance and behaviour in a few pithy sentences that covered a wealth of things unsaid and threatened retribution if she didn't change her ways.

'You know how important this merger with Rochford is to me,' he had raged. 'The day of the little company is over. With Rochford's we'll survive and grow, we'll be set up for life—and I won't have you sabotaging the whole deal with your childish arguments and appalling behaviour!'

Micky had stared up at the stocky, red-faced man in the expensive blue suit, noting absently that her father had put on weight recently, the collar of his white linen shirt was already a shade too tight, and wondered just where her beloved father had gone. What had happened to the unpretentious, hard-working man in his shirt sleeves who had been such a rock to her in her childhood years? This elegantly suited, slightly overweight man before her was so unlike that father that it was as if another spirit had entered the familiar body, driving away the man she knew and loved.

She had entered the dining-room on legs that were not quite steady after the impact of her father's tirade only to find that the seating arrangements increased her tension one hundred per cent. At every other meal, her mother had seated their guest at her side with her husband opposite so that the burden of conversation fell on the two older Dennisons, but this time, to Micky's unadulterated horror, she indicated that her daughter should take the seat next to Adam.

Every fear and suspicion that had been in Micky's mind since she had overheard her mother's comments came flooding back, mixed with a rebellious anger, totally destroying her co-ordination, so that when Adam courteously held a chair out for her she stumbled awkwardly and would have fallen if it had not been for the firm support of his hand that held her and guided her into her seat as if she were a child. Embarrassed resentment made the swallowing of her soup a constant struggle against choking and all the time Micky was painfully aware of the man at her side, knowing that she would have to talk to him at some point—and she couldn't think of a word to say.

Mercifully, for the first half of the meal Adam concentrated his attention on her mother, charming and complimenting her until the older woman was flushed and smiling, her eyes glowing like a young girl's. The brief respite gave Micky time to collect her thoughts, grow accustomed to the fact that Adam was there beside her, and calm herself, waiting until he addressed her directly—because there was no way *she* could initiate any conversation. The few glances she shot at his face, his strong profile firmly etched against the cream wall of the dining-room, gave her no encouragement or help. It was a hard, capable face, but beyond that it gave nothing away.

How old was he? Micky wondered. Her belief in someone of her father's generation had been shattered in the moment he had turned to face her but the formal clothes and the tiny lines around those strangely coloured eyes when combined with his easy, self-assured manner, the confident air of knowing exactly who and what he was, made him seem light-years older than her friends. Beside him, Zac and the others would look mere boys.

'So tell me about yourself.'

Micky started out of her daydream as she realised that Adam had turned and the words had been addressed to her. Hastily she picked up her glass, swallowing a little wine to give herself confidence.

'There's nothing to tell,' she said gruffly.

'Oh, come on!' Adam reproved mildly. 'Your father told me you left school in the summer—you must do something with your days.'

The sudden tautness of her nerves was an instinctive reaction to his question. He had touched on a particularly sensitive topic. Once a week, without fail, since she had left that hated school, there had been some argument with her parents on just this subject.

'I don't *do* anything!' Micky snapped. 'I'm a lady of leisure. Dad has more than enough money to keep me—I don't have to work.'

The last sentence was her father's own words, quoted deliberately, but from the frown that crossed his face she realised that he had taken them as her own opinion. Slight as it was, that frown changed his face completely, wiping away the politely enquiring, almost friendly look in his eyes in a way that made her stomach clench nervously.

'So how do you spend your time?'

'Oh, on this and that.' Micky forced an airy tone. 'I read, I visit my friends, I go shopping—paint my nails.'

An unfortunate remark, that one. It drew those sharp eyes to her inelegant hands and mangled nails.

Automatically Micky hid her hands in her lap, pushing them out of sight beneath the tablecloth.

'Don't you think that's rather a waste?' Adam persisted.

It's none of your business! Micky wanted to retort, but suddenly conscious of her father sitting opposite, very well aware of the fact that she was at last talking to Adam even if his wife's monologue prevented him from hearing what was being said, she forced herself to make a more polite reply.

'I'm not qualified for anything. I made a real hash of my A-levels—failed the lot.'

'So did I—first time. You could always try again.'

'No thanks!' The answer came swiftly, her tone sharpened by memories of the loneliness of the last two years, then, intrigued by his first remark, she went on impetuously, 'Did you really? Fail your exams, I mean.'

Adam nodded silently.

'But why?' He didn't look like a man who had ever failed at anything.

'Oh, the usual reasons. I messed about, didn't work, couldn't see any point to it. Then I got an ultimatum—work or else. I made damn' sure I passed the second time.'

'But you didn't need any qualifications!' Micky protested. He didn't need *anything*; he'd been born with everything—the only son of one of the most powerful businessmen in the country, heir to a fortune from the first second of his life. He didn't even have to work. 'Your father had a job ready and waiting for you.'

Adam's laugh was hard, tinged with cynicism.

'Clearly you didn't know my father. He was the one who gave me the ultimatum—no qualifications, no job. He didn't get where he was by passing out handouts to lame dogs even if they were family. Whatever he gave us we had to earn.'

Automatically Micky noted the use of 'we'. There had been a sister, her father had said, a sister who had died young, but Micky was too busy revising opinions coloured by her father's other remarks to take the point any further. Bill Dennison had been full of stories about this man's life-style, the huge house that had been his father's, the flashy car, the non-stop jetting back and forth between England and the States, that she had assumed he had always been like that.

'Of course it's different for a man,' she said abruptly to fill the silence.

'Why?' The question came sharply, startling her. She had been thinking of her own situation, her father's adamant refusal to let her find a job, particularly the job she wanted. If she had been a boy perhaps it would have been different. As it was, her parents were only concerned that their daughter should grow up to be 'a lady' and that, it seemed, meant doing nothing useful.

'Well—a son would take over the firm,' she mumbled.

'That's a remarkably sexist opinion coming from you. Surely a daughter could do that just as well. Don't tell me you see marriage as the only career for a woman?'

Then, as Micky shook her head confusedly, aware of the fact that she hadn't expressed herself very well and thoroughly disconcerted by the way the conversation seemed to be back to front, Adam putting forward the view that she would have expected to hear herself expressing and vice versa, he persisted almost angrily,

'Is that what you're doing—biding time until Mr Right comes along to keep you in the manner to which you've grown accustomed?'

'No!'

It came out vehemently, her personal feelings intensified by newer concerns. Micky glanced at Adam sharply. Did he know—or guess—what her mother's hopes were? And if he did, would he oppose or agree with them? She knew nothing about his personal life, her father had been reticent on that subject, but she had heard often enough of the energy and determination he put into winning new contracts, finalising deals, and, of course, increasing profits. Would the 'dowry' of the shares in Dennison's that would ultimately come to her be sufficient to tempt him along the road her mother dreamed he would follow?

Suddenly every muscle was tight as a wound spring, the words Adam had whispered in the moment he had helped her to her feet resounding in her head. Clearly her appearance hadn't put him off as much as she had hoped; she would have to resort to more drastic tactics.

'You have a very cynical opinion of women, Mr Rochford, if you think that's all they have in mind!' she snapped, deliberately ignoring his earlier non-chauvinistic comment.

'Do I?'

The changeable eyes were strangely dark in the flickering candlelight, dark and unfathomable, but his response had been given quietly. What did she have to do to provoke him? Adam leaned forward suddenly, his gaze disturbingly intense as if he were trying to probe deep into her mind and read her thoughts.

'Tell me about it,' he challenged softly. 'What is my opinion of women?'

'I don't know!' The swift turning of her father's head in her direction at the sound of her voice made Micky hastily adjust her tone as she went on, 'I've only just met you.'

'That didn't worry you a few minutes ago.' That hard edge to his voice was back, a cold, steely note that she was already over-sensitive to. 'You said I had a very cynical opinion of women.'

'That was because you assumed——'

'I assumed nothing. You're the one making all the assumptions, young lady.'

'Young lady' rankled. It was the sort of phrase her father used when he was laying down the law—she didn't have to take it from this man!

'You said you thought I was waiting for Mr Right to come along!'

'I asked if you were, which is not the same thing at all. Do you always jump to conclusions so quickly?'

Micky shook her head dazedly. She had wanted to provoke him and now it seemed she had succeeded, but she hadn't been prepared for the sudden attack which confused and disturbed her all the more because it had been expressed in a quietly conversational tone with just that hint of ice in his voice to warn her that this was not just dinner-table chat. Even though they were only on the other side of the table, her parents clearly had no idea of the turn the conversation had taken. Her father even directed a small nod of approval towards her at the way she was talking to their guest, some of the tension and anger leaving his face.

'What makes you so sensitive to the subject of marriage anyway?'

Oh, how could she answer that? She couldn't tell him the truth! Her thoughts whirling, Micky blurted out the first thing that came into her head.

'I don't believe in it. It's an irrelevant, outdated institution set up for the benefit of men and to the detriment of women.'

'Which is just the sort of half-baked idea I might have expected you to come up with.'

'Now who's jumping to conclusions?'

Micky reached for her wine and gulped down half of it with a foolhardy lack of concern for the possible effect it might have on her. She felt like a butterfly frantically beating its wings against the hard glass of a window-pane in a desperate bid for freedom. Her eyelids were stiff and heavy from the unaccustomed weight of the elaborate make-up and she longed to rub them to ease the sensation but didn't dare, knowing she would only end up with mascara smeared all over her cheeks.

How had she got herself into this? Her rudeness

hadn't put him off as she had hoped. If anything, he now seemed all the more determined to speak to her, he was ignoring her parents completely and she could just imagine what her mother would read into *that*.

'All right, Mr Rochford, tell me,' she said, feeling a little more confident as the wine took effect. 'What sort of woman do you like?'

And whatever sort it was, she vowed, she would do her utmost to prove herself exactly the opposite.

A slow smile curved Adam's lips but there was no humour in it. It was a mocking, knowing smile that brought no light to those watchful eyes and she didn't like it one little bit.

'Now you don't expect me to fall into that little trap, do you?' he drawled. 'If I describe my ideal woman physically I shall be condemned as some chauvinistic pig who sees women merely as sex objects, and if I say I just like women, full stop, you'll classify me as an undiscriminating lecher. But if I were to tell you that I react to women as individuals—as people—you wouldn't believe me.'

'Why on earth not?'

'Because for some reason, God knows why, you've already decided everything about me—got me filed, classified and indexed under O for Objectionable.'

'Oh, now you're being ridiculous!' Micky declared more forcefully than she actually felt. Adam's words came too close to the truth for comfort. The back of her chair dug into her shoulders, making her aware that she had physically backed away from him as he drove her into yet another corner mentally. How could she ever have considered him even remotely attractive? she thought wildly. That hard, set face hadn't a trace of humanity in it; he looked like a man of stone.

'I'm not blind,' Adam told her coldly. 'I know hostility when I see it—and you're practically eaten up with it. It's there in your face, in your eyes, and it's been there since the moment I first saw you. You looked as if you thought I was about to leap on you and rape you the minute I turned round which, believe me, is not an effect I am used to having on young girls. I've never met you before in my life and to the best of my knowledge I've done nothing that could have provoked such a reaction, so do you mind telling me just what the hell you've got against me?'

Still Adam had not raised his voice, but the savage intensity with which he directed the words at her had Micky springing to her feet, knocking over her chair in the process. As she backed away from him she had a fleeting, blurred glimpse of her parents' faces turned towards her, shock, disbelief, and anger written clear in every line of them, before she turned her attention back to the man before her. She no longer cared what her parents thought, she only wanted to make it clear to everyone present that she disliked this man intensely, that they could forget once and for all any hopes they might have of her ever even considering the idea of marrying him.

'I'll tell you what I've got against you, Mr High and Mighty Rochford! I don't like your sort—and I don't like you. You think of nothing but money, you must have made your fortune three times over but still you want more—you haven't got the faintest idea what it's like not to have your wealth and your advantages! You're sitting here at my parents' table, eating their food and being oh so polite—but would you have come if there'd been no Dennison's to take over? Would you have come in your flashy car with your flowers and your compliments if Dad had been still just Bill Dennison, jobbing electrician?'

'Michaela, that's enough!' Mr Dennison roared, moving swiftly round the table towards his daughter, but Adam stopped him by the simple expedient of putting out an arm to block his path.

'No, it's not enough,' he said in a voice tinged with such deadly menace that Micky's blood turned cold at the sound. 'It bloody well isn't good enough,' he went on, his eyes like hazel chips of ice fixed firmly on Micky's flushed face. 'There's more to this than you're saying and I want it all—I want the truth!'

'The truth!' Micky spat the words at him, all trace of reason wiped from her mind. 'You want the truth, all right, you can have it! I was happy—we were happy—the way we were until we became involved with men like you and your father, until money became the only thing that mattered. I've watched my parents crawl to people like you—and why? Because you mean *money*—and quite frankly it makes me sick!'

'And——' Adam said implacably as she paused for breath.

'And . . .' To Micky's horror sobs threatened to choke her as she struggled to get the words out. Tears were trickling down her cheeks, trailing black rivulets of mascara with them, but she didn't care. 'And I wouldn't marry you if you were the last man on earth! Even if you do want my money.'

That stunned him. He stared at her, total incomprehension stamped clearly on his face. Micky heard her mother's appalled gasp, saw the horrified look that passed between her parents and, knowing that she had burned her boats once and for all, turned and fled from the room.

A miserable, sneaking sort of wind whistled down the street and tugged at Micky's jacket so that she shivered and hunched her shoulders against the cold. It was a rotten spring, in fact it had been a long, hard winter altogether. The house in which she shared a tiny bedsitter with Susie was only a hundred yards down the road but still she lingered in spite of the cold, studying the gardens around her, noting the buds on the trees, the green noses of tulips and daffodils poking above the dark earth, and here and there a tiny carpet of snowdrops or a brave display of purple and gold crocuses brightening the dullness, offering a promise of better days to come. At home Arthur would be busy in the greenhouse, sowing bedding-plants ready for the first hint of summer.

Micky shook herself hard. She had to stop thinking of her parents' house as home. It wasn't home to her any more; she hadn't set foot in the place for over five months.

'Your friend called again,' Susie announced before she had even taken her coat off.

'Friend?' For a second Micky was confused, then realisation dawned and she scowled. 'Not again!'

''Fraid so—but honestly, Mick, I can't understand why you're so reluctant to see him. If I had a gorgeous man like that after me I'd want to encourage him.'

Micky's scowl darkened. 'Adam Rochford isn't *after* me—at least not in the way you mean.'

'Then what *is* he after?'

'I don't know,' Micky admitted defeatedly. 'But whatever it is, he's not going to get it.'

'Well, I don't think he's the sort to give up easily,' was Susie's wry comment. 'This is the third time he's been round this week—I'm running out of stories to explain why you're not here.'

Micky nodded glumly, her thoughts elsewhere. She was only too well aware of just how many times Adam Rochford had called at the flat, every occasion was etched in her brain, and the most vivid memory of all was that first evening when she had arrived home, worn out after a hard time at work.

'You've had a visitor,' Susie had announced. 'A man—no, not Zac,' she had added hastily, seeing the dawning hope on Micky's face. 'Someone I've never seen before, but I'd like to see a lot more of him.'

'Who?' Micky was confused. She and Susie shared the same crowd of friends, there was no one she knew that Susie did not.

'He didn't leave a name, said it didn't matter, but he seemed to know a lot about you.'

'What did he look like?'

'Tall, very sexy, with hair the colour of conkers in autumn if you know what I mean.'

Micky nodded slowly, her stomach lurching queasily. She knew exactly what Susie meant and there was only one man who immediately fitted that description, a man with hair of burnished chestnut and cold, changeable eyes. A dull ache of fear started up inside her.

'An older man—light brown eyes—very smooth and expensively dressed, probably in a flashy suit?' she asked, her voice rising and falling unnaturally.

'Sounds like him.' Susie nodded. 'But he wasn't that old——'

'Old enough!' Micky snapped. To her horror she was trembling all over. How had Adam tracked her down? She had only been in this flat for a few weeks—and what did he want? Why had he come after her now? Why couldn't he leave her alone?

'I don't want to see him!' she had declared fiercely, stunning Susie. 'Not ever, do you understand? If he comes again you don't know where I am—don't tell him where I work—and if he calls when I'm at home then don't let him in. I don't ever want to see him again!'

'Okay, okay, I get the message,' Susie laughed. 'But don't get things out of proportion, it might just be a one-off call. Perhaps he won't come back.'

But Adam had come back, not once but six times all told, most of them at the times when Micky was out at the nightclub where she worked as a waitress. But there had been one horrific occasion when he had called when she was in the flat. She had spent an almost unendurable five minutes crammed up against the wardrobe listening to that deep, smooth voice with the faint American drawl to it, as Susie tried to convince him that she was not at home, terrified that he might insist on coming in to wait until she got back. He had gone away that time and for a few days they had been left in peace. Micky had begun to relax again, to believe that, frustrated in his attempts to see her, he had finally given up, but Susie's announcement tonight had proved that hope just a delusion.

Unwillingly Micky's thoughts went back to the night five months before when the tension between her father and herself had finally come to a head, the resulting explosion devastating her life completely, and anger burned deep in her heart at the recollection of Adam Rochford's part in those events.

It had been a week after the dinner party, a week which had seemed more like a year to Micky who had lived through a nightmare, each day worse than the one that had gone before it, filled with endless rows, non-stop argument and criticism and finally deteriorating into a state of uneasy tension in which her parents hardly spoke a word but still managed to convey their condemnation simply by their silence. She hadn't seen a friendly face all week and had hardly been out of the house in that time. Her father was determined that she would apologise to Adam for the things she had said and Micky was equally adamant that she would not. The result was an ugly stalemate that was slowly destroying her so that when Zac arrived unexpectedly—and illegally—at the house while her parents were out she had greeted him rapturously, pouring out her troubles to him.

Zac's response to her story was a string of angry curses, his fury mixed with a frank amazement that she should tolerate the situation at all.

'You're letting them run your life,' he had declared. 'You should tell them to go to hell and get out now.'

'But where would I go?' Micky sounded forlorn and a smile touched Zac's mouth, lighting his handsome face.

'You could move in with me. Any time you like, Mick, you've only got to say the word.'

'I—I don't know,' Micky managed. It was too big a step, she didn't know if she was ready for it.

From the very first night she had fallen head over heels in love with Zac, entranced by his devil-may-care attitude. Something that made her feel this good, this happy, *couldn't* be wrong, so it wasn't any sense of morality that held her back but the knowledge of her own inexperience, her ignorance of just what physical lovemaking entailed. Oh, she knew the factual details, of course, her mother had made sure of that, but only in a clinical, impersonal way, totally divorced from any sense of the *loving* that had to go hand in hand with the physical actions, and when she had reached the age when she might have asked questions for herself as adult to adult, the changes had already begun and her mother had moved away from her into another world.

'Mick?' Zac was kissing her now, his lips soft against her throat. 'What about it, honey? We could have some great times together.'

Micky sighed. It *was* an answer. She could be free of this house that no longer seemed like a home, free to be with someone who cared for her—and she loved Zac. If things had been different she would have overcome her nervousness in time but now she had to decide before she was quite ready. She wanted to be with Zac, but could she uproot herself again and move into the tiny flat he shared with three friends? It ws a huge leap from their free-and-easy relationship to that sort of commitment and it scared her.

Zac's arms slid round her, drawing her close, and she abandoned herself to his embrace, drawing comfort from his closeness.

'Kiss me,' she whispered, her voice quavering on the words.

His lips were warm and firm and she felt her fear melting away under them and in the release from the tension that had gripped her responded with an intensity that was quite unlike her usual shyness, arousing an immediate response in Zac. His hands went to the buttons on her dress, unfastening them swiftly, his hand slipping on to the warm softness of her breast.

'Your parents and this Rochford will destroy you between them,' he muttered. 'You're young, you should live *now*.'

'I know,' Micky choked, closing her eyes as his caresses soothed her. 'Oh Zac, I know—but——'

'But what? For God's sake, Mick, you don't fancy that bloody Rochford, do you?'

'Fancy him?' Micky's voice was thick with revulsion. 'No! How could I? He's much too old and he's an opinionated, arrogant bastard. I don't *fancy* him—I hate him!'

A faint sound brought her eyes open on the last words and her attention was caught by some movement glimpsed vaguely over Zac's shoulder. As her gaze focused fully she saw that the door was open and lounging in the doorway, an expression of cynical amusement on his face, was Adam Rochford himself.

Micky froze, her hands stiffening on Zac's shoulders, her eyes widening in shocked horror. When Zac sensed the tension in her he swung round to discover the cause of it, his movement exposing her to the full force of those appraising eyes, revealing her unbuttoned blouse and the soft curves of her uncovered breasts. She saw Adam's amusement fade, to be replaced by a scathing contempt that seemed to sear her skin with its intensity. Her cheeks coloured hotly and she felt physically sick.

'Good afternoon, Miss Dennison.' Adam's urbane greeting was very much at odds with the coldly burning disdain that made his eyes look almost translucent. 'I apologise if I've intruded on something important, but your father was under the impression that you would be alone.'

'My father?' Micky gasped through lips that were suddenly dry and stiff. 'Is he with you?'

'He's just putting the car away,' Adam informed her

calmly. 'He told me to go on ahead but I expect he'll be here any minute, so . . .'

His eyes dropped from her burning face to her disarranged clothing then swung back up again, his meaning unmistakable, but as Micky lifted shaking hands to refasten the buttons Zac recovered from his surprise and lurched to his feet in a violent movement.

'Now look!' he exploded furiously. 'I don't know who the hell you are, but——'

He stopped dead, silenced by the look in those icy hazel eyes.

'No, we haven't met before,' Adam's voice was cold and hard as steel. 'But believe me, Mr Hamer, I've heard a great deal about you.'

Micky's hand stilled on her dress as she stared at Adam, her mind reeling. Mr Hamer, he had called Zac. How did he know that? What *had* her father told him?

'But as I have the advantage of you,' Adam continued smoothly, not giving Zac time to recover from his use of the other man's name, 'allow me to introduce myself. My name is Rochford, Adam Rochford.'

A slight twist to his mouth, the faint sardonic emphasis on his surname revealed to Micky more clearly than if he had actually told her in so many words that Adam had caught Zac's 'bloody Rochford' as he came in—and if he had heard that then—oh God, how much had he heard?

'So you're Rochford.'

With half her mind Micky noticed the way Zac's hands were clenched at his sides, and knowing his uncertain temper she shivered at the thought of the consequences if he lost control.

'Zac——' she began but he brushed her interjection aside.

'So you're the great Adam Rochford,' he flung at Adam. 'Well, let me tell you that I've heard a lot about you too, and none of it complimentary.'

The glance Adam slanted in Micky's direction left her in no doubt that he knew where those reports had come from and he had more than likely heard her own angry words about him. She didn't care, she told herself. She had meant every word of it—but that didn't stop her from wishing the ground would open and swallow her up.

She couldn't believe this was happening, it couldn't be true, she thought frantically, her eyes going back and forth between the two men in front of her. They were about the same height but somehow Adam seemed to dwarf Zac and the contrast in their appearance couldn't have been greater if it had been deliberately planned. The younger man's scruffy denim jeans and tumbled mane of curls looked thoroughly disreputable beside the immaculately tailored lines of another of those suits, a fawn one this time, worn with a bronze-coloured shirt that picked up the lights in Adam's smoothly combed hair. He looked sleek and powerful and as predatory as a hunting tiger, Micky thought with a shiver.

'And I don't give a damn who you are,' Zac was saying. 'Because nothing gives you the right to barge in here like this.'

'Nothing,' Adam agreed with deceptive smoothness. 'Except that, unlike you, I have the invitation of the owner of the house—and really you only have yourself to blame if I "barged in" as you put it. If you indulge in your sordid little affair in the most public room in the house you really can't be surprised if someone interrupts things. Tell me,' he went on, leaning indolently back against the wall and folding his arms across his broad chest, 'is this how you usually carry on in someone else's home? Because if it is I'm hardly surprised that you're not exactly welcome.'

'It's none of your bloody business!' Zac's grip on his temper was loosening rapidly. 'Micky can do what she likes. She's not a child.'

'No?' Adam looked sceptical. 'I suppose it depends

on how you define the term.' His eyes swung to Micky's face, watching for a moment as the colour came and went in her cheeks. 'In my book she is a child because she can't see through your nasty little game.'

'Why, you——' Zac lost control once and for all. He launched himself towards Adam, his fist raised high.

'Zac, no!'

'What the hell is going on?'

Micky's cry of panic clashed with her father's angry shout from the doorway in the same moment that Zac's fist landed on Adam's jaw with a sickening thud. Even in the middle of an unbelievable nightmare like this, Micky had to admit to admiration for the way Adam reacted to the powerful blow. He took just one involuntary step to the side then immediately regained his balance, drawing himself upright, his eyes glittering with cold anger.

'*Not* a clever move, Mr Hamer,' he said on a menacing note of warning. 'I'd advise you not to try that again.'

'He won't get the chance,' Micky's father stated firmly. 'I want you out of this house, young man—*now*!'

As Zac hesitated, his eyes going from Adam to her father and back again, Micky found that the panic that had held her frozen had ebbed at last. Heedless of her gaping dress, she sprang to her feet.

'You can't do that! I won't let you. If Zac goes I go too!'

The sudden whitening of her father's face almost destroyed her but she held firm to her resolve. He wouldn't let her go. They had fought before, though, admittedly never as badly as this, and he had always come round in the end. He'd let them both stay and that would show Adam Rochford just where he got off!

She couldn't believe it when her father looked away from her, turning towards Adam as if seeking his advice. Through a haze of shock she saw the younger man's eyes rest on her face, narrowing thoughtfully, and then his head moved in a coolly decisive nod.

'No!'

But Bill Dennison ignored Micky's outburst as he turned back to Zac.

'Out!' he repeated in a tone that brooked no further argument, amd Zac shrugged indifferently.

'I wouldn't have wanted to stay anyway,' he blustered with some attempt at bravado before stooping to pick up his jacket from the settee.

'Dad, please,' Micky tried again.

'*You* can stay, Micky.'

'I won't—not without Zac.'

'I'm afraid you can't stay with him,' was her father's weary response.

Micky knew she had no choice; she couldn't back down now. Wrathfully she turned on Adam who stood, unmoving, a silent observer of the scene before him, his face an impassive, stony mask. Without his intervention her father would have let her stay.

'I hope you're happy!' she spat at him. 'I hope you realise just what damage you've done to our family—and I pray you never forget tonight, because I promise you I never will!'

Not a muscle moved to betray what he was thinking, only those watchful hazel eyes followed her as she walked towards the door behind Zac. And all the way down the hall she could feel them watching her still, burning into her back until she felt that she was branded with their imprint for life.

CHAPTER THREE

VERY slowly Micky came back to the present to find that her hands were twisted nervously together in her lap. That night had destroyed the relationship between herself and her parents finally and, it seemed, irrevocably. She had neither seen nor heard from them since then, and the one small fact that tempered the pain of that separation in the slightest way was that if she didn't see her mother and father, then at least she was also spared another confrontation with Adam Rochford—or she had been until now.

What was she going to do? For some private reason of his own Adam was hounding her. It was getting so bad that soon she would be afraid to answer the door because how long would it be before he came when she was here on her own, with no Susie to act as a defensive barrier? Micky started violently as Susie thrust something at her.

'He left a note this time.'

Micky stared at the crisp white envelope her friend held out to her, eyeing it warily as if afraid it might bite. It was completely blank, not even her name marred its clear surface. Hesitantly she took it and slid her finger under the flap, shocked to find that her hands were shaking uncontrollably as she took out the single sheet of paper. She felt as if she were handling a live bomb, one false move and it would blow up right in her face. Unfolding the paper she stared blankly at the brief message.

'What are you afraid of?'

That was all, just those five curt words written in a firm, clear hand, the black ink standing starkly against the white paper. There was no preliminary greeting, no signature, clearly Adam Rochford didn't bother with such forms of politeness, and the absence of his name implied an assumption that she would know only too well who had sent the note—which, of course, she did.

With a violent movement Micky crushed the note in her hand, flinging the crumpled ball of paper in the vague direction of the wastepaper bin.

'Damn him!' she cried furiously. 'Damn, damn, damn Adam Rochford and his type!'

Hot tears burned her eyes, but even as she blinked them back she had to admit to herself that she didn't know if they were tears of anger or sheer blind desperation.

The café was warm, almost too warm, but Micky shivered convulsively as she picked up her cup and sipped gratefully at the strong, sweet coffee, feeling its warmth seep through her. The cup was already half empty; she was going to stay just as long as it took to finish this one drink and then she was going, in fact it was all she could do not to turn tail and run right this minute. If he didn't come soon—— Her hand jerked uncontrollably, clattering the cup against the saucer as she replaced it on the table.

Perhaps it had been the wrong idea to get here early. She should have known that every minute she spent waiting would stretch out to infinity, draining her confidence with every second that passed. But she had wanted the slight advantage that being the first would give her, knowing she couldn't cope with arriving and finding him waiting. She couldn't have walked across the room towards him knowing that those cold eagle's eyes were watching her as they had done on that hateful night all those months ago. Micky shivered again in recollection and made a move to get to her feet then sank back with a tiny moan of despair. She had to stay, had to see him, or Susie would never forgive her.

If the first three weeks had been bad then the last fortnight had been hell. Adam had called every single day and once or twice there had been occasions when she had been alone in the flat and hadn't dared to open the door when the bell rang, convinced it had to be him. No one else she knew would have put their finger on the bell and left it there, the shrill sound echoing round and round the small room until she was ready to scream. The first time she had actually gone to the window and looked out, seeing the sleek, silver-grey car pull away from the kerb, but then the thought that he might have seen the movement of the curtains and, knowing she was there, might come back again, had her stumbling back against the wall in a panic.

Susie had stood it for so long but two days ago she had issued an ultimatum. Either Micky agreed to see Adam or she would force her hand.

'I've had enough, Mick,' she complained. 'I've spun him every yarn in the book and I know he doesn't believe any of them, and quite frankly I'm sick of it. If you don't want to see the guy then tell him to his face. But don't ask me to do your dirty work any more. The next time he comes I'm going to let him in and that's final!'

Which was how Micky came to be here in this small, scruffy café, a rapidly cooling cup of coffee before her, waiting for Adam Rochford. She had asked Susie to say she would meet him here for two reasons, the most important being that she couldn't bear to have him in her room. Tiny as it was, the bedsitter she shared with Susie was all the home she had and she hated the thought of Adam setting foot inside it so she had chosen the neutral ground of the coffee bar.

The very faintest of smiles touched Micky's lips as she surveyed the other occupants of the café—a couple of building-site labourers relaxing after work, their hands and clothes still covered in dust, a tramp who had been lingering over a single cup of tea even longer than Micky herself, and, in the corner, a group of teenagers dressed in a weird and wonderful assortment of the very latest street fashions. In his immaculately tailored suit Adam Rochford would stand out like a very sore thumb indeed which was how she had planned it, grasping at the straw of putting him at a very slight disadvantage.

As for Micky herself, she considered her blurred reflection in the steamed-up window and grinned. Oh yes, she'd had fun preparing for this meeting once she'd accepted that it was unavoidable. Adam was prejudiced against her already, he would expect to find an outrageous, punkish creature and that was just what he would find. The vivid pink and black striped sweatshirt worn with skin-tight purple jeans would hit him as soon as he walked into the café and she had echoed the gaudy colours in her make-up. Her hair hadn't had the attention of a hairdresser in months and it hung in a shaggy mane around her face. Only last week, in an attempt to drag herself out of the black mood that was the direct result of Adam Rochford's persecution, she had experimented with a colourant, hoping for a warm, coppery effect. The result had not been quite what she had expected but the bright auburn certainly fitted with the image she wanted to project today.

But Micky's grin faded again as she met the eyes of the girl reflected in the window. The over-bright colour of her hair contrasted savagely with the shadows under her eyes, the result of endless sleepless nights. She had lost weight too, and the baggy sweatshirt swamped her slender figure, hanging loosely around her thin waist and hips. Three months of not eating, not sleeping, had stripped away the gamine appeal of her features, leaving them gaunt and pale so that her high cheekbones seemed etched starkly on her narrow face, the bright blue of her eyes dulled with unhappiness. There was a new look about them, one of disillusionment and loss of innocence, that made her glance away swiftly, glad to be distracted by the sudden opening of the café door.

The sight of a tall dark figure in a scruffy denim jacket set her heart beating painfully so that she lowered her eyes again, staring fixedly at the table-top. It wasn't Zac, she told herself fiercely, forcing a rigid control on her feelings. She was well past the stage of hoping to see him, hoping he would say it had all been a mistake and he still cared for her, but just the sight of anyone remotely resembling him revived the feelings of bitterness and disillusionment, leaving her painfully vulnerable. She couldn't afford to feel like that now; she needed all her strength to face Adam Rochford and she couldn't let her memories drain away what little she had left. Zac had taken too much from her already; taken everything she had to give and thrown it back in her face.

Micky pushed her empty coffee cup away from her restlessly. She didn't want to stay any longer but she was afraid of what would happen if she didn't. If Adam arrived and she wasn't here, then surely his next move would be to drive straight round to the flat.

A swift glance at her watch made her frown. Six o'clock, she had said; it was almost half past now. She wasn't going to wait any longer for a man she didn't want to see! She was leaving—and to hell with the consequences! Pushing back her chair in a sudden rush of anxiety to get going, she bent to pick up her handbag from the floor.

'Running away?' a cool voice asked from somewhere above her.

Startled, Micky froze, still in her awkward, crouching position. Her eyes focused on a pair of elegantly booted feet and long legs in brown cord jeans. Then, as she slowly straightened up, her gaze moved over an oatmeal heavy-knit sweater topped with a tan leather jacket and up until it met a pair of eyes the colour of a fine dry sherry that were regarding her with a mocking amusement.

This couldn't be Adam Rochford! The thought sounded in her head so clearly that she had to bite down hard on her bottom lip to stop the words actually slipping out. This wasn't the man she remembered! He looked like his own younger brother, like a man much nearer her own age than the sleekly-suited businessman who had been in her mind. She didn't remember him being quite so arrestingly handsome either—but the voice was the same. She remembered that mocking intonation only too well—and she could never forget those eyes.

'As a matter of fact I was going to get another coffee,' she lied with a stiff little gesture towards her empty cup.

'Well now, you don't have to bother,' was Adam's comment as he placed two full cups on the table. 'I assume you do take milk?'

Micky could only nod, too busy with her own thoughts to speak. So much for having the advantage over him by getting here early! He had still crept up on her unawares and she felt thoroughly disorientated by his sudden arrival and altered appearance. She had been nervous enough before, but the shock of realising that Adam Rochford was a singularly attractive man drove every last trace of her hard-won composure from her mind and left her struggling with an almost uncontrollable urge to turn and run.

'Well, sit down,' Adam said quietly enough but with a hint of impatient command that squashed all thoughts of escape and had her sliding unwillingly into her chair as Adam seated himself opposite, one hand toying idly with his spoon, his eyes fixed on her face.

Micky clasped her own hands together on the top of the table and stared at them fixedly, not wanting to look at Adam. The knowledge that he was studying her made her stomach clench in nervousness and dislike and she couldn't make herself lift her head to meet the scrutiny of those searching eyes. He could make the first move! she thought rebelliously. She hadn't wanted this meeting and she was damned if she was going to start the conversation!

Out of the corner of her eye she saw the long fingers leave the coffee spoon and drum impatiently on the table, the slight noise jarring unpleasantly on her already hypersensitive nerves. What *was* he thinking? What did he want?

She started nervously as her cup was pushed towards her, still without a word being spoken. Automatically her hand moved to push it away again and in that moment she glanced up, catching the reproving frown her unthinkingly petulant gesture had earned her. For a second their eyes locked together, Micky's openly rebellious, Adam's thoughtful and considering, then at last he spoke.

'You might as well drink it—I bought it for you,' he said mildly.

'And you'd hate to see your precious money wasted!' Micky snapped, nervousness sharpening her tongue.

'You don't improve on acquaintance, do you?' was the sardonically murmured response, then he disconcerted her completely by adding, 'you're painfully thin. Are you eating properly?'

'That's none of your business!' Micky flashed defiantly. 'I eat what I want—and anyway Zac likes me slim!'

'Ah yes, the aggressive Mr Hamer.' Adam's eyes darkened suddenly and he touched his jaw thoughtfully as if remembering Zac's fist against it. 'How is he?'

Micky scowled down at her coffee, cursing her own thoughtlessness that had led him to that question. She didn't want to talk about Zac—couldn't talk about him. For one thing she doubted if she could say anything without breaking down. Bitterness welled up inside her as the memories she had struggled to hold back earlier threatened to swamp her. She wasn't part of Zac's life any more, had never really been part of it. She was just another girl to him, a passing fancy, someone to take to his bed—she wasn't fool enough now to call it making love, though, for her, that was what it had been. Over the past long, lonely months she had managed to grow a delicate new skin over the raw wound Zac had inflicted on her, but Adam's casual words had ripped it open again. She had brought in Zac's name as a deterrent, a defence, and now it had rebounded savagely on her.

'He's fine,' she growled ungraciously, but then her head came up again sharply. The mention of Zac had thrown her, she was letting this man get to her. It was time she started holding her own.

Suddenly, seeing Adam sitting there, relaxed and totally sure of himself, Micky was overwhelmed with a burning fury of hatred. She hated him for speaking Zac's name, for reviving memories of events that had almost destroyed her, and most of all she hated him for being a man and so able to take his sexual pleasures casually and carelessly, with no commitment, then walk away without a second glance as Zac had done. Anger at the thought and a determination not to let him see her own private pain drove her on to the attack as she demanded, 'Just what is all this about, Mr Rochford? You've been harassing me for weeks, calling at the flat day and night in that flashy silver car of yours——'

She broke off abruptly at the mocking lift of an eyebrow.

'So it was you at the window that time,' Adam drawled. 'Why didn't you open the door?'

'Because I didn't want to see you! I should have thought that was obvious. I'm only here now because I can think of no other way to get you off my back. So tell me, just what do you want?'

'To see you.'

The mildly spoken reply was not at all what she had

expected. Micky could think of no reason at all why this man should want to see her. Abruptly she reached for the rejected cup of coffee and gulped some of it down, grimacing as she tasted it. Adam slid the sugar bowl towards her.

'Why does that upset you so much?'

'I'm not upset!' Micky protested, the vehemence of her words contradicted by the distinct tremor of her hand as she spooned sugar into her cup, scattering grains across the table as she did so.

'Would it help if I said your parents had asked me to come?'

The quietly spoken question stilled Micky's hand, her fingers clenching tightly over the spoon.

'My parents!' she echoed shakily, unable to suppress the note of longing in her voice. It had been a long, lonely five months without any contact with her mother and father. 'You're here because my parents asked you to come?'

Adam nodded slowly and Micky was intensely aware of that keen hazel gaze on her face, noting every fleeting expression.

'And because I felt responsible,' he said soberly.

'Responsible?' Micky shook herself mentally. She was beginning to sound like a parrot, repeating everything like this! 'Responsible for what?'

'I hate to see a family split down the middle by some silly little feud,' was Adam's response, but Micky hardly noticed a new intensity in his voice, was scarcely aware of the way he had sidestepped her question because she was thinking back to what he had said earlier and a bubble of anxiety rose up inside her, catching in her throat.

'Why did Mum and Dad ask you to come?' she asked sharply. 'Is something wrong?'

'Not a thing,' Adam assured her, and Micky was stunned to catch a hint of sympathy in his voice. Was it her imagination or had there been the tiniest flash of warmth in those cold eyes? 'Nothing's wrong. They're both fine.'

Micky sank back in her chair, suddenly painfully aware of the fact that her fingers were still grasping the sugar spoon tightly. With an effort she forced them open, letting the spoon fall on the table with a distinct clatter. Released from the tension of worry for her parents, she suddenly felt desperately homesick. There were dozens of questions she wanted to ask, small, trivial questions, but ones that were vitally important to someone deprived of contact with her family—but she couldn't ask them, not of this man. Her one aim in meeting Adam Rochford like this had been to impress on him the fact that she was handling her life perfectly well and that she resented him interfering in any way. She couldn't afford to show any sign of weakness; if she did he would never leave her alone.

'Well, you can tell them I'm fine too!' she declared with an attempt at insouciance that didn't quite succeed, coming out as brittle indifference instead. 'Was there anything else you wanted to know?' she went on stiffly. 'My flatmate will be wondering where I am—I said I'd be back by seven. After all, I did ask you to be here at six.'

The firm mouth twisted slightly at her return to the attack, but whether in amusement or annoyance Micky couldn't quite judge. Whatever his reaction was, it had destroyed any sympathy he might have felt. The warmer light had faded from his eyes, leaving them cold and unfriendly as before.

'So I was late,' he murmured sardonically. 'I apologise—but if you're going to arrange a meeting in some obscure little place like this the least you can do is to make allowances for the problem of negotiating the traffic on my way across town.'

Adam's words stung. It wasn't so much what he had said, more the reminder of the world to which he belonged and which she had rejected; the world on the other side of London; a world of money and expensive cars that was light-years away from the Rio coffee bar. She glanced across at the man sitting opposite, recalling her original aim in choosing such a place for their meeting and an irrational anger sparked in her at the realisation that she hadn't really succeeded.

In the more casual clothes, his hair tousled by the wind, Adam blended in with his surroundings quite easily. It was true that the leather jacket was of a distinctly better quality than anything any of the other customers were wearing but even so he was no longer the smoothly affluent business man of the night of that appalling dinner party. It was impossible not to notice that two of the girls from the group in the corner had been eyeing him with blatant appreciation since the moment he had walked in, casting envious glances in Micky's direction from time to time, and it was equally impossible to be surprised at their reaction. Seen like this, Adam seemed so much younger, more approachable—— Her mind clamped down on that train of thought. Approachable implied she wanted to get closer and that was not how she felt at all.

'I accept your apology, Mr Rochford,' she said tightly, using the formality of his full name deliberately as much as a defence against her own thoughts as from a need to warn Adam to keep his distance. 'But the fact remains that I must be going, so if there's nothing else——'

She made a move to get to her feet but stopped with a small cry of shock as a hand snaked out and caught her wrist, imprisoning it in a bruisingly powerful grip.

'Oh no you don't, young lady! It's getting to be a habit of yours, running away when the going gets tough. This time you're not getting away with it.'

Those hazel eyes were just chips of ice in Adam's hard, set face—and only seconds before she had been thinking he looked almost approachable! Micky nearly laughed out loud at the thought, but Adam's next words drained any trace of amusement from her mind.

'You're going to stay right here until I say you can go,' he stated implacably. 'I want to talk to you.'

'We've been talking—for nearly half an hour,' Micky pointed out with deliberate rudeness. 'And you haven't said a word that interests me in any way whatsoever, so if you don't mind——'

She made another attempt to move then winced as the grip on her wrist tightened painfully, warningly. Mutinously she slid back into her seat.

'So talk,' she muttered sullenly.

Only then did Adam release her hand and she snatched it away as soon as the pressure eased, cradling it with the other as if his touch had actually burned her.

'What do you want to talk about?' she demanded a moment later when Adam didn't speak and the silence between them threatened to grow unnerving.

'You.'

The single syllable seemed to shiver in the air between them, bringing Micky's head up swiftly. She had no intention of revealing anything about herself to this man—he had no right to pry into her life!

'No chance!' she declared adamantly, and saw his carelessly indifferent shrug.

'Your parents then?' he suggested as if offering a compromise, but Micky was not deceived by the conciliatory note in his voice. She didn't know if he had seen the loneliness and longing she hadn't been able to hide earlier, but she rather suspected he had—and she wasn't going to be caught like that again.

'What about them?' she asked without interest.

'They're worried,' Adam stated starkly. 'Have you any idea what they've been through since you walked out? Did you ever stop to think of the unhappiness and anxiety your petty little gesture brought them?' He leaned forward suddenly, well and truly on the offensive now. 'Would it have been too much to ask to let them know where you were?'

'They knew where I was!' Micky cried, her rising voice drawing several curious glances. 'I left to be with Zac,' she added more quietly, almost choking on the words.

'I know that!' Adam dismissed her protest contemptuously. 'But you didn't stay with him, did you? You staged your childish little tantrum and walked out of their lives without a thought for how they might be feeling. It's been nearly six months and not a word or a phone call in all that time. They didn't even know if you were alive!'

'Well, they know now!' Micky retaliated desperately, thrown off balance by the fact that he knew she had left Zac. *How* did he know? And, worse still, what else did he know? Her involvement with Zac had been a mistake, how great a mistake she had only realised when it was over, but she had gone into it in all innocence, believing in her feelings, thinking them to be right. But, seeing her actions through the eyes of this sophisticated, worldly man, she felt suddenly tainted and unclean. She could well imagine how he would view her behaviour, reducing it to the 'sordid little affair' he had so scathingly called it on that last night in her parents' house.

This was how she had felt at that dinner, she recalled, driven into a corner with her back up against a wall, unable to think of anything beyond this hateful man and the detestable things he was saying. 'You've seen me. You can tell them I'm alive!'

'Tell them yourself.'

The curt command hit Micky with a force that was almost physical, combining with her private pain to drive the breath from her body so that her response came out in a strangled gasp.

'I—I can't.'

'Why not?' Adam snapped. 'Too proud? Too

stubborn? Too damn' bloody-minded? What would it have cost you to make one small gesture—a card at Christmas perhaps?'

Micky winced as that savage tongue lashed her, re-opening a scarcely healed wound. Christmas had been a desperate time, a black, desolately lonely time that had driven her to make the long trek across the city, walking for miles in the bitter cold to stand outside her parents' house, staring forlornly at the lighted windows from the opposite side of the street and wishing she had the courage to cross the road, walk up the drive and ring the doorbell. But the knowledge that she would not have been able to bear it if her father had opened the door and she had seen not welcome but hostility on his face had kept her frozen to the spot. When she had turned away at last it had been like being torn in two, as if she had left part of herself behind, and an echo of that pain rang in her voice as she lashed out wildly.

'Why should I? Did *they* make any gesture? Did they contact me or send a card? Why didn't they make some effort to find me if they were as worried as you say?'

'Because I told them not to.'

The flatly spoken statement had the effect of a slap in the face, clearing Micky's thoughts and bringing a vivid mental picture of the last time she had seen her father on the day she had walked out. She had declared her intention of leaving with Zac, believing, *hoping* that her challenge would not be taken up—and her father had turned to *Adam*, seeking his advice and——

Micky's dislike of Adam crystallised into a savage, blinding hatred as she recalled how it had been his coldly decisive nod that had encouraged her father to persist in his determination to expel Zac and, by association, Micky from the house. Since that time she had spent days, weeks, waiting for some sign of reconciliation from her parents, her unhappiness growing with each day that passed and none ever came—and now she knew why! Her blue eyes blazing fire, she rounded on Adam.

'*You* told them!' she cried, oblivious of the now undisguised interest of the couple at the next table. 'How *dare* you! What right have you got to play God like this—who gave you permission to interfere in my life? I thought your father was bad enough, but you're in a class of your own!'

That got a reaction—not a pleasant one, Micky admitted to herself, seeing Adam's face harden perceptibly, but at least it was better than that immovable, unfeeling calm. A small sense of triumph at having rocked him at last released the last restraint on her tongue.

'Do you enjoy messing up other people's lives, breaking up families? Is that how you get your kicks? Don't you have enough fun just making your millions?'

Cold, stony eyes never left Micky's face as she paused for breath.

'Finished?' Adam asked and the mocking condescension in his voice sparked off another furious outburst.

'No, I haven't finished!' Micky injected every ounce of the loathing she was feeling into her voice, her anger fuelled by the irrational thought that if Adam had not forced that final showdown with her father then she would not have been pushed into a decision she wasn't ready to make, a decision that had left her wide open to the pain and disillusionment that Zac had inflicted on her.

'I have just two more things I want to say: One, you are the most hateful, detestable monster I have ever had the misfortune to meet; beside you even a boa constrictor would look attractive! And second, this is the last time you interfere in my life! I thought I hated you before but I didn't know what the word meant until now. You disgust me! I can't stand the sight of you—and if I never see you again it will be too soon!'

Again came that indifferent, dismissive shrug of those powerful shoulders and there was even a glint of cruel humour in the cold, light eyes.

'Then I'm afraid you're going to be disappointed,' Adam said, the steely note in his voice twisting Micky's stomach into knots. 'Because it's only fair to warn you that if you persist in refusing to listen to reason, you're going to see a great deal more of me.'

'If listening to reason means dancing to your tune, then I'd sooner die!' Micky spat at him. 'So *you* be warned, Mr High and Mighty Rochford—if you plan to change my mind you're in for a very long and very hard fight indeed!'

The smile that crossed Adam's face turned her blood to water and she shivered as she saw the light of battle burning deep in his eyes.

'Is that a challenge, Miss Dennison? Because one thing you ought to know about me is that I can never resist a challenge—I always take it up—and when I do, I invariably win.'

CHAPTER FOUR

'It's a nasty night out there, love,' the doorman at Garbo's commented as Micky pulled on her coat. 'Are you sure you don't want me to call you a cab?'

'No thanks, Joe.' Micky smiled her gratitude. 'I can't afford one. I've got my umbrella, that'll keep me dry.'

'It wasn't just the weather I was thinking of,' Joe told her seriously. 'I don't like to think of you walking home alone,' he added, concern showing on his round, lined face so that Micky felt tears prick at her eyes. She always seemed to be on the verge of tears these days, especially if someone showed any kindness. Really, it was most unlike her.

'Don't worry,' she reassured Joe as confidently as she could, 'I'll be fine—and I won't be alone, I'll have an escort.'

Which was about the only way to describe it, she added wryly to herself on her way out of the door. She managed a jaunty little wave before she turned her attention to the street, frowning against the darkness as she fumbled with her umbrella, trying to make it seem as if putting it up was her only reason for lingering on the top step. In reality her eyes were scanning the street, checking the row of parked cars, looking for one particular vehicle.

Surely he hadn't given up, not so soon? Micky felt almost disappointed; she had expected much more of a fight than this. No, there it was, parked perhaps fifty yards away, the silver-grey colour looking slightly eerie in the darkness, like a ghost car—no, a shadow, she told herself, smiling at the image, a silent, persistent night-time shadow, always with her like her own physical shadow in the daylight. Well, she knew the routine by now.

Strolling down the steps with a carefully assumed air of nonchalance, Micky headed into the driving rain, hearing the powerful engine start up behind her, and a moment later the sound of tyres splashing through the puddles told her he was behind her once more, slowing the car to a crawl so as not to overtake her. That had frightened her at first, she recalled. Until she had realised that it was Adam's car the sleek, purring shape behind her, following close at her heels, had been distinctly unnerving. It was almost as if the car had taken on a life of its own and become some sort of predatory, metallic hunting cat.

Micky allowed herself one swift glance over her shoulder just to check it was *the* car; it wouldn't do simply to assume it was. Garbo's wasn't in the most salubrious district and it was just possible that she had picked up a genuine kerb-crawler. A faint, wry smile touched her lips at the sight of her 'escort'. As always, the car was in total darkness and, blinded by its headlights, she could not make out the driver's face, but she knew very well who was there. The smile widened at the thought of what a policeman might make of the sight—really, Adam had been very lucky so far. She wondered just what explanation he would give for following her if he was ever stopped.

Adam! Micky pulled herself up short. These late night walks home with Adam Rochford in attendance had become so familiar, so routine, that even though she hadn't spoken to him since the evening in the café she had fallen into the habit of thinking of him by his first name. She'd have to watch that if she ever spoke to him again.

But in a crazy sort of way she had been talking to him over the last ten days, holding imaginary conversations in her head with the man in the car behind her; it was the only way she could cope with his persistent, unwanted presence once the first fierce determination not to let him see she had even noticed had worn off. The temptation to stop and look back, to shout, to stand still and refuse to move until he left her in peace had been almost irresistible but she had known that it would have been playing right into Adam's hands.

If she reacted at all she would show that he was getting through to her and that was something she was resolved she would never do so she had talked to him in her mind, starting with angry railing at him for his harassment, dredging up every insult she could think of and wishing she could actually speak them out loud to his face. That had satisfied her for a day or two but gradually the enjoyment of being rude had worn out and she had progressed to a calmer, more reasonable attitude, phrasing and rephrasing the questions she wanted to ask to discover just why he was hounding her like this, but all the time knowing that she would never dare ask those questions of Adam himself.

Strangely enough, she had come to find Adam's presence almost comforting. It was something she could rely on, something dependable, and there had been little enough of that sort of thing in her life just lately, so that in a perverse sort of way she would miss him if he ever stopped—*when* he stopped, she corrected herself firmly. He would give in before she did. For one thing, trailing her like this, night after night, must be almost doubling his petrol bill—and playing havoc with his social life, she added with a private smile at the thought of how Adam's lady friends might react to that.

There were girlfriends, she knew that now. From not being able to bear to hear Adam's name she had swung suddenly to the realisation that if she was to put up any sort of fight against him she would have to know what sort of man he was when he wasn't tormenting her. In order to fight fire with fire she had asked around to see if anyone she worked with knew of him and had found one other waitress whose father and brother were both employed at Rochford Electronics. Hazel had been able to supply her with one or two interesting facts, notable among them being the presence of several particularly glamorous women in Adam's life, women he had been seen with at all the right places, but not, she assured Micky, the women he would ultimately marry. It was rumoured on the factory floor that Rochford's managing director set particularly high standards for the sort of woman who would become his wife. Old John Rochford had impressed upon both his son and daughter the necessity of marrying someone who would add lustre to the family name, and so far no one had even come close to qualifying as a suitable candidate. Remembering her father's comments on the subject, Micky could well believe that this would be the case. Her secret smile widened at the possibility that the beautiful Miranda—or Julie—might be neglected as a result of Adam's late night vigils outside Garbo's.

A sudden flurry of rain slashed against Micky's face in spite of the protective shield of the umbrella, making her shiver. April showers indeed! This was a full-scale typhoon! Resentment flared at the thought of the man behind her, safe and warm inside his car, and her steps mirrored her anger as she marched around a corner and straight into a wind that, channelled between the houses, had turned into a gale. The force of it swung her small, slight body round, turning her umbrella inside out as it did so.

Cursing aloud, Micky struggled with the recalcitrant object, battling vainly against the wind. Blinded by the rain, she was dragged a yard or two along the street, staggering slightly as the gale buffeted her. At last she flung the ruined umbrella from her in disgust, swung round to face the right way again and marched forward straight into a lamp-post hidden in the gloom.

Her head hit the concrete with a sickening thud, red sparks exploded in front of her eyes and she reeled uncontrollably, her eyes tight shut against the pain. The wind caught her and swung her round again, knocking her several steps backwards. She felt the edge of the pavement, twisted her ankle awkwardly, lost her balance and with a high-pitched cry of panic fell straight into the path of the silver-grey car.

Dimly she heard the screech of brakes; her hip hit the bonnet with a force that jarred every bone agonisingly, and then she was lying full-length on the hard surface of the road with a sharp pain in her left knee and a hazy red blur where her mind should be.

A car door slammed, hasty footsteps approached and seconds later warm, strong arms closed around her shoulders lifting and supporting her. In the instinctive reaction of panic she clung to them, not daring to open her eyes, muttering incoherently, 'Help me—please—help.'

'Hush,' a quiet, comforting voice soothed her, one that in her confusion and pain she couldn't quite place. 'It's all right, Midge, calm down. You had a nasty fall but you'll be okay in a minute. I'll just——'

He moved as if to leave her and Micky reached out blindly with a cry of fear, Gentle hands eased her clutching fingers open.

'It's all right, I'm not going anywhere. I just want to get you off the road. Can you stand?'

Micky shook her head miserably. She didn't want to move. Then at last she opened her eyes and looked dazedly up into the face of her rescuer, into his eyes that were as dark as forest pools in the lamplight, dark with concern and sympathy.

'Try, Midge. I'll help,' the attractive, soothing voice urged, and looking deep into those eyes, drawing the strength and encouragement she needed from what she saw there, Micky nodded slowly.

'I—I'll try.'

With his hands under her arms almost lifting her bodily from the ground she managed to stagger to her feet then sagged exhaustedly against the hard strength of the man beside her. His arms came round her again as she clung to him, too shocked to speak or even to cry. Her head was spinning. She felt sick and totally disorientated.

'Can you make it to the car?'

The voice was familiar, Micky thought confusedly. She *knew* that slightly accented attractiveness, had heard it before, but there was something very new about it, something that made it totally strange and unfamiliar. Moving like an automaton, acting only on the urging of that voice, her mind still too numb to think about what she was doing, she put her right foot forward then her left and cried out sharply as her knee jarred painfully.

Instantly she felt the strength of those warm arms swing her off her feet, carrying her towards the car. Seconds later she was leaning back in a soft upholstered seat, resting her aching head against it with a sobbing sigh of gratitude and relief. Very vaguely she heard the other door open and sensed a warm body slide in beside her.

'Are you okay?' that naggingly familiar voice asked and a hand touched her cheek very softly. 'Poor little girl,' he murmured. 'You really shook yourself up.'

The gentleness of his tone broke down all that was left of Micky's self-control and as weak, exhausted tears coursed down her cheeks she had no strength to fight them back.

'Oh, Midge!'

Once more she was gathered into the comfort of those arms, cradled against the firm wall of his chest, her cheek against the softness of wool, and it felt right to be there, warm and safe and infinitely reassuring. A hand stroked her hair gently, soothingly, until her sobs slowly eased, quietened and eventually ceased on a final gasping sigh.

'Better now?' the low voice asked and as the haze of shock cleared from her brain she felt she could almost remember where she had heard it before—almost but not quite.

'Thank God I was only crawling,' he said fervently. 'Things could have been a hell of a lot worse if I'd been travelling at any speed.'

At his words the last of the mist that had been clouding Micky's mind cleared suddenly and her head snapped up in shock, her whole body tensing and pulling away as it came home to her just whose car she was in, whose voice that was, whose arms held her. Those arms tightened briefly as if to restrain her but then, seeing the look on her face, Adam released her abruptly.

'There's nothing to be afraid of,' he said a trifle sharply, then as Micky sank back in her own seat he went on, 'how do you feel now?'

How *did* she feel? Hazily Micky tested her physical condition; her mental state was quite beyond her. Her hip ached, her left knee throbbed and she was shivering violently.

'Shaky——' she managed. 'And cold——' Her voice shook on the last words as the shivering increased and she could not have said if it was a reaction to her accident or to the other, more emotional shock of finding herself held close in Adam's arms.

'Here.' Adam was shrugging himself out of his thick sheepskin jacket. When he laid it over her Micky had no strength to protest but clutched the coat to her, huddling into it thankfully. It was still warm from the heat of his body and smelt faintly of some tangy cologne and a deeper, more personal scent that she found strangely comforting. In that moment she felt she would fight anyone who tried to take the jacket from her.

But Adam showed no sign of wanting to retrieve his coat as he leaned forward to turn his key in the ignition, flicking a switch to set the heating system going as he did so.

'The car will soon warm up, you'll feel better then. I'd better get you home so I can check you over, find out just what damage you've done to yourself.'

Home. The word echoed in Micky's still dulled brain. She thought longingly of a comfortable bed, hot sweet tea, and her mother's anxious concern then stiffened as the truth came home to her. Not *that* home! She had forfeited her place there long ago. Adam meant her flat—and she had no intention of letting him in there!

'No!' she cried sharply. 'No—I don't want—I—Susie will be asleep,' she finished desperately.

'Well, I'm not leaving you till I've made sure you're really okay,' Adam stated firmly. 'So where do you want to go?'

I want to go *home*, Micky thought miserably but she couldn't frame the words. For one thing, she couldn't just turn up at her parents' house like this, not in the middle of the night and in such a state.

'I don't know,' she admitted defeatedly.

'Micky!' Adam sighed his exasperation. 'We have to go somewhere! For one thing, I can't stay here, I'm parked on a double yellow line as it is, and the police aren't going to like that if they spot us.'

Micky scarcely heard him. The warmth of the jacket around her was soothing; the shivering had stopped and her mind drifted tiredly. She just wanted to sleep.

'Police,' she murmured vaguely, the word stirring a memory of her thoughts just before the accident. 'What would you have done if the police had seen you following me?'

Adam laughed, shaking his head at the inconsequence of her question.

'Don't worry, I had my story all ready.'

'You would have.' It was just a whisper. Heavy waves of tiredness were washing over her and her eyes were closing again. It was so much easier to give in, not to fight it.

A tiny part of her mind heard Adam's muffled curse then the engine roared into life as the car swung away from the kerb. The movement roused Micky slightly and as she stirred she felt a warm dampness trickling down her left leg. Shifting awkwardly in her seat she moved the jacket aside and peered down at it.

'Adam!'

Her sharp cry brought his head swinging round in the same instant that, acting on high-speed reflexes, he brought the car to a halt.

'I'm bleeding!' Micky announced in a voice that was filled with blank amazement. She pointed to the red line that ran down her leg, thick and sticky underneath her tights, and watched Adam's face grow grim as he followed the direction of her finger. 'It'll ruin your coat,' she added shakily, overwhelmed with embarrassment at the thought.

'What the hell does that matter?' Adam growled roughly. Turning in his seat he tucked the jacket more closely round her with swift, impatient movements that were none the less comforting for all their brusqueness. 'Just relax,' he ordered. 'We'll get that seen to.'

The softness and warmth of the sheepskin lining seemed to cocoon Micky from reality. Her leg didn't matter, her aches and bruises didn't matter, nothing mattered—Adam would see to everything. As the car moved forward again she roused herself very slightly.

'Where're we going?' she asked drowsily and heard his murmured response through a head that seemed to be full of cotton wool, catching the word 'flat' and nothing more. Reassured, she closed her eyes. Her flat would do. Susie would forgive her if they woke her up—and then she could sleep. She could leave it all to Adam; she trusted him implicitly. Her eyelids drooped and a welcome oblivion closed over her.

Swamped by sleep, Micky scarcely registered the moment when the smooth movement of the car finally ceased. She had a vague sensation of being lifted, felt the chill wetness of rain on her cheeks, causing her to turn her face into the shelter of Adam's chest once more, then she drifted away again rousing only when she was lowered on to the softness of deep cushions.

She frowned petulantly, murmuring a complaint as her coat was eased from her but when firm hands moved under her skirt, pulling at her tights, she jolted wide awake, panic-stricken and fighting.

'What the hell do you think you're doing!'

'Calm down, little girl,' Adam's voice was firm. 'I want to see to your leg and I can't do that while you're wearing these.'

One hand pushed her back against the cushions, but Micky jerked up again, protesting furiously.

'Don't touch me! I'll do it! I—oh!'

Her eyes widened in shock as she saw her blood-smeared leg and the raw gash on her knee. The sight made her stomach lurch queasily, draining her of the strength to argue so that she lay back and let Adam complete his task, closing her eyes in a fury of embarrassment.

'I'll get some water and clean it up a bit,' Adam said as he straightened up. With a swift glance at her ashen face he went on reassuringly, 'Don't worry—it looks worse than it is. I don't think you've done any real harm, but you've certainly bled like a pig. Once we've washed the blood off we'll be able to see what we're dealing with. I won't be a minute—but don't move.'

Don't move! Micky thought satirically as Adam left the room. Nothing was further from her thoughts. She felt as if she would never move again. Every bone in her body ached, her muscles screamed a protest if she so much as shifted position, and her head was pounding sickeningly. She must look a sight too. Lord knows what Susie had thought when Adam turned up with her looking like this!

Susie! Micky frowned her confusion. Where was Susie? Surely her friend could have helped her with her tights, sparing her the embarrassment of having Adam remove them. It had to be at least one in the morning, she hadn't left Garbo's until after twelve—Susie couldn't still be out, could she?

Micky stared up at the ceiling, wondering, then froze. That clear, fresh cream paintwork wasn't even remotely like the dull, faded blue of the ceiling in the bedsitter! And the dark brown settee on which she lay was as alien to her as if it had just landed from Mars.

With an effort she levered herself into a sitting position and stared around her, her eyes opening wide in stunned disbelief as she took in a large, spacious room decorated in earthy colours of brown, rust and cream. A warm, friendly sort of room, though it would look even better if there were a few plants about the place, she noted automatically—but one she didn't know; had never seen in her life before.

The door opened again and Micky rounded on Adam as he came back into the room carrying a tray.

'Where am I? I don't know this place! Where have you brought me?'

'Steady on.' Adam's voice was pitched at the quiet, controlled level one might use to soothe a highly-strung thoroughbred racehorse. 'I told you I was bringing you to my flat, remember—in the car,' he added as Micky shook her head.

'I thought you said *my* flat! I can't stay here! I don't want to be here.'

'Michaela!' Adam's tone had sharpened perceptibly. 'Calm down! You've had a nasty shock, and getting hysterical won't help matters.'

'I'm not hysterical!'

'Don't you ever stop fighting?' Adam sighed, banging the tray down in exasperation. 'Look,' he went on in a coldly reasonable voice. 'You were hurt, in shock, and in no state to be left. You adamantly refused to let me take you to your flat so I brought you here.'

'But I——'

'All I want to do is to bathe that leg of yours and get you into some sort of better shape then I'll take you home.'

'Home?'

'To your flat, if that's what you want.'

Every word was spoken slowly and clearly; he might have been explaining to a difficult and not very bright child. There was no hint of reproach in his voice, but all the same Micky felt reproved as she saw the sense in what he had said. She *was* over-reacting, reading more into the situation than was actually there. In the car she had felt she could trust him—but then in the car she had been exhausted and shaken, very vulnerable and hopelessly dependent on Adam. Still, so far he had shown her nothing but kindness.

'Sorry,' she said stiltedly.

'Forget it,' was the curt response. 'Here, drink this.'

Micky regarded the glass he held out to her with suspicion, her nose twitching warily.

'Brandy?' she queried and at his nod she frowned. 'I don't like brandy.'

'Give me patience!' Adam exploded. 'Michaela Dennison, do you ever do anything without arguing?'

'Well, Mum had a difficult time having me—they thought I wouldn't survive,' Micky told him candidly. 'So Dad always said I was born fighting and I——'

She stopped abruptly, silenced by the pain of loss that tore through her. With a brusque movement she snatched the glass from Adam's hand and took a large gulp.

'Not like that!' Adam declared furiously. 'It's meant to be medicinal. I don't want you roaring drunk!'

For a moment their eyes clashed over the rim of the glass, Micky's mutinous, Adam's coldly clear. Then, very slowly, Micky raised the glass again and took a small, delicate sip. Adam's mouth twitched in dry amusement at her exaggerated concession to his instructions and unthinkingly Micky smiled back at him, her eyes lighting in response. But the smile was wiped from her lips when Adam's next move was to turn away and pick up the bowl of water from the tray. Involuntarily she stiffened as he knelt on the floor, tensing in anticipation of his touch.

But it was not the ordeal she had anticipated. After the first stinging shock of antiseptic on the raw grazes Micky found she actually enjoyed the experience. Adam's movements were sure and capable, his hands amazingly gentle, and the warmth of the water was a balm to her wounded skin. It was a relief to see that, as Adam had predicted, once the mess of smeared blood had been wiped away, cuts and deep grazes were the majority of the damage though her knee looked puffy and swollen and the skin was already discoloured on one side. Adam's long fingers probed the heated flesh delicately, and he frowned swiftly at Micky's sharply indrawn breath.

'That hurts? Can you bend it?' Then, as Micky did so, trying unsuccessfully to suppress a grimace of pain, he nodded slowly. 'It'll be hellishly sore tomorrow, I've no doubt, but I don't think you've broken anything.'

He glanced up suddenly, warm hazel eyes looking straight into Micky's anxious blue ones as he smiled reassuringly.

'Don't worry, kitten, you'll live.'

Micky's breath caught in her throat. She felt as if her heart had suddenly stopped then jerked back into action again, beating far more swiftly than before. She couldn't believe the transformation that one brief smile had wrought on the hard-boned face before her. This was the man she had dismissed as 'quite attractive', she thought wonderingly, but when that smile lit up his face the description was woefully inadequate. He was stunningly, devastatingly handsome, and with that thought came the equally shocking realisation that she wanted very much to kiss him.

But Adam had moved, shattering the moment. Micky watched speechlessly as he got to his feet, seeing him clearly for the first time that night. For the life of her she couldn't drag her eyes away from the vivid, glorious colour of his hair, the lean, lithe body, the powerful shoulders and chest under the heavy cotton shirt and narrow hips and long, long legs encased in tight denim jeans. He had legs up to his armpits, she thought on a grin—a grin that faded swiftly as Adam swung round to face her.

How old *was* he? It seemed impossible that she had ever considered him middle-aged, and the thought of lumping him in with her father's generation was positively laughable. He had a young man's body, strong and firm, without a trace of the excess weight that was already blurring the outline of so many of her father's colleagues.

Memories of the way she had been cradled against that hard length, her hands clutching at Adam's arms, assailed Micky, making her head whirl crazily. She felt hot and then cold at the thought of how she had wanted to kiss him, at the recollection of how, only moments before, this diabolically attractive man had been kneeling at her feet, sponging blood and grime from her muddy legs with the gentleness of a trained nurse. Her conscience pricked her savagely at the realisation that never once had she offered a word of gratitude for all he had done to help her.

'Mr Rochford,' she began hesitantly, using the stiffly formal term of address in order to distance her thoughts from the unexpected and disturbing path they had been following. She almost faltered when she saw the swift dark frown that crossed his face at her words, but forced herself to go on. 'I—just want to thank you for looking after me like this—I don't know what I'd have done without you.'

A faintly rueful smile chased the frown from Adam's face.

'Without me, you wouldn't have been in this mess,' he responded gravely.

It was the first reference that either of them had made to what had actually happened and Micky shifted uneasily in her seat, remembering that, for all his kindness, Adam was still the same man who had been harassing her, following her night after night. The thought drove away the sudden attraction she had felt towards him, leaving her feeling lonely and uncertain and not at all happy about being alone with him any longer.

'I think I'd like to go home now,' she said tightly.

But it wasn't as easy as that. When Micky got to her feet it was to find that her injured leg had stiffened underneath her, putting any weight on it was an impossibility, and even with Adam's help walking was agonising. She made it as far as the hall but after three steps down the thickly carpeted carridor, half walking, half carried, she slumped against the wall, her lips pressed tightly together to suppress the moan of pain that almost escaped her.

'I—I can't,' she gasped, all her strength leaving her so that she collapsed on a crumpled heap on the floor.

Adam swore violently, bending down to scoop her effortlessly from the floor. Expecting to be carried back to the settee she had just left, Micky lay passively in his arms, too tired to struggle or even care, but Adam walked past the living-room, kicking open a door further down the hall and pressing the light switch with his elbow before he moved into the room and deposited her carefully on the wide double bed.

It took perhaps five seconds for Micky's pain-blurred brain to register that she was in a bedroom, and another five or more to realise that, from the uncompromisingly masculine décor, this could be none other than Adam's room, but after that her reaction was instantaneous. Sitting up, she tried to swing her legs over the side of the bed, fighting back the whimper of pain the movement brought to her lips.

'What the hell are you doing now?' Adam demanded impatiently.

'I'm not staying here! I don't know what you're up to, but I'm not——'

'I'm not "up to" anything!' The attractive, low-toned

voice had vanished completely, replaced by cold, clipped tones that were tight with suppressed anger. 'For God's sake, child, are you incapable of seeing reason?'

'Child' stung, sparking Micky's volatile temper.

'Reason! I can see only one reason for you to bring me in here, and——'

Micky broke off, stunned by Adam's laughter.

'Oh, so that's it? You're terrified that I might have designs on your virtue. Well for your information, you misguided infant, nothing was further from my thoughts. You can't walk; you have to sleep somewhere tonight—and this happens to be the only bed available. I'm stuck with you and that's all there is to it. I have no intention of forcing my attentions on you, whatever that suspicious little mind of yours may be thinking. To be perfectly honest, you're not my type. I prefer my women to look like women.'

'But isn't there any way I can get home?' Micky persisted, choosing to ignore his last uncomplimentary remark and the slighting 'infant', even though a sharp stab of anger told her that Adam's barbs had hit home. The last thing she wanted was to be thought Adam Rochford's 'type'!

Adam shook his head firmly.

'You could carry me.' It was not a suggestion that appealed—to either of them probably—but it was better than the thought of staying here. If she got back to her bedsitter then she would at least be free of him; there would be no tomorrow morning to face.

'No chance,' was the adamant reply. 'In case you hadn't noticed, Miss Dennison, it's almost three o'clock. I've been up since six this—yesterday morning and I have to be at work again in just over five hours. I have no intention of spending any of that time carting you half-way across London. I've done my share of carrying you tonight and, believe me, for such a little scrap of a thing you're no featherweight. So will you please just stop fighting for once and get into bed like a good girl, then we can both get some sleep.'

Still Micky hesitated. There was nothing to be gained by any further argument, she admitted to herself, but that didn't make it any easier to give in and do as he said. She was achingly tired and the bed looked comfortable and welcoming, but she was distinctly apprehensive about the prospect of waking up in it in the morning. Tonight Adam had been amazingly kind and—at the beginning at least—incredibly gentle, and she was intensely grateful for his help. But would that gratitude be enough to enable her to cope tomorrow—or, rather, later today—when she very much suspected that the temporary truce between them would be forgotten and Adam returned once more to the offensive? She didn't know what to do, but when Adam spoke his words made up her mind for her.

'You have two alternatives,' he drawled mockingly. 'Either you agree to get into that bed now, without any further argument, or I'll undress you myself and put you in it.'

And having no doubt at all that he meant what he said, Micky could only concede defeat and choose the less ignominious course of action. But as she undressed slowly and awkwardly, her injured leg hampering almost every movement, she resolved that just as soon as it was humanly possible she was getting out of this place. She had wanted no contact with Adam Rochford, but fate had been against her and circumstances had forced them together—but she wasn't going to stay a moment longer than she actually had to!

The bed was warm, soothing her aching body, the soft pillows cushioning her throbbing head, but still Micky found it hard to fall asleep. She squirmed angrily at the memory of that disparaging 'I like my women to look like women', and was stunned to find that the thought brought a dull ache of—it couldn't be disappointment? She didn't *want* to be the sort of woman who would attract a man like Adam Rochford!

Or did she? Remembering that irrational longing to kiss him, Micky was forced to wonder if she really knew *what* she wanted. Not that it really mattered anyway, she told herself realistically, that strictly formal 'Good night Miss Dennison' as Adam had left the room told her exactly where she stood in his eyes. But he had used her Christian name once or twice earlier and before that, in the car, he had called her something else, something that had sounded almost friendly. What was it he had said? Sleep claimed her before she could remember.

CHAPTER FIVE

'YOU did what?' Micky's voice sounded shrill and harsh but she was too angry to care or even notice. 'You did *what*?' she repeated, flinging the words at the man before her, her eyes flashing fire.

Apparently completely unmoved by her fury, Adam simply repeated unhurriedly and indifferently the words that had sparked off this particular attack of temper.

'I rang that sordid little nightclub where you work and told them you wouldn't be in tonight or any other night this week—if at all.'

'You had no right——'

'Someone had to tell them,' Adam pointed out with cool reasonableness. 'See sense for once, child. It'll be a week at least before you're moving round on that leg with any degree of comfort, let alone waiting on tables. You'll have to rest.'

None of which she was arguing with, Micky admitted privately. If she had had any illusions on that score then the effort it had cost her simply to make the journey from the bedroom to the living-room of Adam's flat had swiftly revealed the truth. Even the slightest movement sent a shaft of pain through her injured knee, the skin of which was now mottled with a lurid collection of bruises in livid reds and purples. There was no way she could hope to be able to get to work, let alone function in a job that kept her on her feet for six hours. Given time, she would have rung Danny, the manager of Garbo's, and told him herself. Now the matter had been arbitrarily taken out of her hands, but it was the high-handed way in which it had been done and in particular those final words 'if at all' that had set a light to her anger.

'I'm quite capable of taking care of myself,' she began again in a cold proud voice, determined to refute that condescending 'child'. She was eighteen, damn it, not eight—and she'd found that job for herself, without any help from anyone. 'You may have lost me my job through your interference and work isn't exactly thick on the ground right now. Even you must know that! I realise that what I earn must seem like a drop in the ocean to you, but I *need* that money!'

Adam's shrug implied total indifference to her plight. 'I'll find you a job,' he said smoothly. 'There must be something going at Rochford Electronics with better pay and far more social hours.'

'I wouldn't work for you if you paid me!' Micky snapped tartly, quite forgetting in her fury that that was exactly what he had been proposing.

'Do you enjoy being a waitress so much then?'

'No.' It slipped out before she could stop herself. Sordid little nightclub, he had called Garbo's and if she were honest the description was pretty accurate. She didn't enjoy being a waitress, in fact she positively disliked being shut away in an artificially lit, smoky, noisy room for hours at a time, but it was *her* job, proof of her independence, and knowing Danny she doubted that he would hold the job for her even for the week she might be off. It seemed as if every time Adam came into her life something went terribly wrong.

'I don't want your job! I don't want anything from you! What do I have to do to convince you of that?'

Then, because he seemed about to answer and because the glint in his eyes warned her that she wasn't going to like what he said, she added hastily,

'And now I'd like to go home, please. Susie will be getting frantic. She's probably got the police out looking for me.'

'No, she hasn't,' Adam countered blandly. 'When I called at your flat this morning she was still asleep—she hadn't even noticed that you hadn't come home.'

Thanks, Susie! Micky thought bitterly. She could have been kidnapped, could be dead, and no one would know. It was ironical really, so many times in the past she'd argued with her parents over just this issue, insisting on her right to come and go as she pleased without having to declare her destination or the time she would be back, impatient at what she saw as their petty, narrow restrictions. Now the realisation of just how alone she was and what might have happened made her feel cold all over, so that she saw that concern in a very different light, a light that coloured her reaction to Adam too.

Suddenly Micky was very much aware of the fact that if Adam had taken her at her word when she had told him to leave her alone then she *could* have been alone, hurt and needing help last night. The accident had nothing to do with Adam, it had been the result of the appalling weather and could still have happened if he hadn't been there. Overbearing and arrogant as he was, he had helped her and she had shown him precious little gratitude.

'Would it be possible for you to drive me back to my flat?' she asked, carefully keeping her voice at a level of neutral politeness. 'I'm sorry to impose on you any more, but I really can't manage on my own.'

One eyebrow quirked upwards sharply in frank surprise at her change of tone but Adam met the conciliatory gesture more than half-way.

'No trouble,' he assured her smilingly. 'But it can wait half an hour, surely. I don't know about you, but I could murder a coffee. Have you had anything to eat?'

Micky could only shake her head. She wished he wouldn't do that! It was unnerving the way he could switch from the arrogant, domineering creature she detested to a man with an easy charm and a smile that would melt a far harder heart than her own. That smile might conceal a multitude of sins, but it made her want to forget the devil underneath.

'Sandwiches okay?' Adam was saying. 'I'm afraid

there isn't much else—I wasn't exactly expecting company.'

'A sandwich would be fine,' Micky agreed.

As Adam turned towards the door the puzzle that had been nagging at the back of her mind suddenly surfaced so that she blurted out her question impulsively.

'Why do you live here? I mean——' she added hastily, seeing his uncomprehending frown '—I thought you inherited that monstrous great place—your father's house.'

'Oh, that.' Adam dismissed his father's luxurious mansion with a wave of his hand. 'What would I want with a great barn of a place like that when there's just me? Besides, it doesn't belong to me now. When my father died I gave it to my sister's husband, he lives there with his daughters though even with the three of them it's still three-quarters empty. And I quite agree with you,' he added disconcertingly, 'it is a monstrous great place.'

The door had swung to behind Adam before Micky quite realised she was still staring. Slowly she sank down on to the settee, sighing with relief as she took the weight off her bruised knee. If she hadn't been so angry earlier she doubted that she could have made the effort to get to her feet in the first place—and now that she came to think of it she was ravenously hungry, which was hardly surprising when she considered that it was well after noon.

The flat had been disturbingly silent when she had finally surfaced from her exhausted sleep and when she checked her watch it was to discover that she had slept for nearly eight hours. That explained the silence; Adam must have left for work while she was still asleep. She had pulled on her jumper and skirt, grimacing at the dark, muddy patches that stained both items, and slowly and painfully made her way to the living-room, abandoning a half-formed idea of leaving before she had to face a further confrontation with Adam as soon as she put her foot to the floor. She had been lying on the settee, wondering what on earth she was going to do, when the banging of a door had announced Adam's unexpected return.

Micky frowned thoughtfully, puzzling over Adam's last remark. Once she had started thinking clearly again, refreshed by her long sleep, it had surprised her to find that, contrary to her preconceived image of him in his father's luxurious house, he in fact lived in this flat—a one-bedroomed flat, she added, remembering how he had told her that his was the only bed available. Not only that, but it now appeared that he had given away the huge mansion—none of which fitted with the idea she had had of him.

Micky winced inwardly as she recalled Adam's scathing comment about the speed with which she jumped to conclusions, and her frown deepened. If she had had the only bed in the place then where had Adam spent the night? A swift glance round the room, revealing a pile of neatly folded blankets unnoticed until now, gave her her answer.

Oh Lord, he must have loved that! she thought on a wave of hot embarrassment, giving up his bed to her and having to make do with the couch. Not that it seemed to have done him any harm. Considering that he must have had four hours sleep at most, he looked disgustingly wide awake and, of course, impeccably groomed in yet another of those dark, expensive suits. Physically he looked very different from the casually dressed man who had come to her rescue the night before, reverting once more to the sleek businessman she had disliked on sight.

It was this change in Adam's appearance that had made her feel uneasy and on edge when he had first arrived so that Micky had finally exploded at his comment about her job. But now that she had calmed down she saw that in reality the difference went far deeper than any superficial matter of externals. Last night had altered their relationship subtly but irrevocably. After that shocking moment of realisation when she had seen him once and for all as an incredibly attractive man she could no longer revive the feelings of hatred and repugnance she had had towards him in spite of the fact that she still deeply resented his interference in her life.

Shifting slightly to ease her leg, Micky considered the room once more, her gaze automatically drawn to a framed photograph that stood on a bookcase. She had noticed it earlier but had been too preoccupied with her own thoughts to give it much attention. Now she studied the smiling, glowing face of the dark-haired woman with more than a passing curiosity.

Which of Adam's women friends was this? She must be someone rather special to have her photograph so openly displayed. She was certainly beautiful—very much Adam's 'type'.

Micky flinched as a shaft of something that felt unnervingly like envy shot through her. It couldn't be! There was no earthly reason for her to be jealous of any woman Adam liked. She frowned at the photograph. There was something about it that was familiar, reminding her of someone.

'That's Nina.' Adam's voice broke in on her thoughts and Micky's head swung round to face him.

'Nina?' she questioned blankly, for Adam's tone had implied that she would know the woman's identity.

Adam nodded slowly, his attention apparently fixed on the coffee he was pouring. Without needing to be told he added two spoonfuls of sugar to the cup and stirred it before handing it to Micky, an action that she found thoughtful and considerate. It showed that he had noticed little things about her and remembered them. But then the thought of just how many things those observant hazel eyes might have noticed, things she hadn't wanted him to see, brought a wave of uneasiness, so that she affected an excessive interest in the bubbles on the surface of her coffee and almost missed Adam's next remark.

'My sister Nina,' he said, and something in the quiet voice brought Micky's eyes back to his face, catching the fleeting flash of raw emotion in his expression. He covered it pretty quickly but Micky had seen it, a hint of an old pain, a remembered sorrow, and her heart twisted in sympathy as she recalled how her father had said that Adam's sister had died young. The girl in the photograph was so lovely, so *alive*—it didn't seem possible.

'How did she die?' She had blurted out the words before she realised how appallingly stark and brutal they sounded. 'I'm sorry—I——?'

Adam lifted a hand to silence her.

'It's okay. I'd planned on telling you,' he said in a voice that was quiet and calm, but with that revealing second of emotion still in her mind Micky was sensitive to every subtle nuance of his tone and she caught the fractional unevenness that spoke of something he found difficult to remember. Her conscience pricked her uncomfortably. Adam had always appeared so confident, so sure of himself, that she had never stopped to consider any more personal feelings he might have. It was less than a year since his father had died. Micky shivered; it would take her a long, long time to recover from a loss like that.

'Nina was seven years older than me,' Adam said slowly. 'When she was twenty-three she met Gerry and fell in love with him. Gerry's a doctor—a wonderful, caring, intelligent man—but he's Nigerian.'

He paused, not looking at Micky but staring straight in front of him, frowning darkly at his memories.

'They got engaged, wanted to marry as soon as possible. Gerry was so right for Nina, he made her ecstatically happy and any fool could see that he was crazy about her, but my father couldn't see past the colour of his skin. He played the heavy father, threatened, shouted, refused to let Gerry into the house. He even tried to stop the wedding.'

Micky's eyes went back to the smiling face of the girl in the photograph. She felt a deep empathy with Nina Rochford. It had hurt so much when her parents had opposed Zac's visits to the house so she knew how the other girl must have felt. How she wished that for one of them it could have worked out! But Adam had spoken of his sister's *husband* so at least Nina had married her Gerry, while Zac had never even loved Micky; he had simply used her and then discarded her. Forcing her mind away from thoughts that were too painful to form, Micky turned back to Adam—a new and very different Adam and one she wasn't quite sure how to react to.

'But they did marry?' she prompted, and received an abstracted nod in response.

'They married, but my father refused to attend the wedding. He raised hell when he found out that I was there and after that he refused to have anything to do with Nina. He rejected her completely, wouldn't see her if she came to the house, tore up her letters without reading them. He even tried the age-old trick of cutting her out of his will—not that that mattered a damn to Nina—or Gerry—but his coldness almost broke her heart. When her first child was born she tried to see him to heal the rift, and again when she had the second little girl two years later. She wanted him to know his grandchildren, wanted them to know him, but he wouldn't *give*!'

Adam's hands clenched suddenly on the edge of the coffee-table, his knuckles showing white.

'He was a stubborn old bastard, too bloody proud to admit he'd been in the wrong. When he had his first heart attack six years ago, the doctors didn't expect him to live. Nina drove down from Birmingham to be with him—she never arrived. Her car collided with a lorry on the motorway, she was killed outright.'

The last bleak words fell starkly into the silence and Micky could find nothing to say in response. Something she had heard Adam say on that evening in the coffee bar echoed round and round in her head, gaining a new importance with every repetition. 'I hate to see a family split down the middle by some silly little feud.' At the time she hadn't been able to see why it should matter a damn to him what happened between herself and her parents, but his story had changed all that.

Suddenly Micky felt icy cold. How would she feel if something happened to her mother or father while she was alienated from them like this? Adam had accused her of being too proud and stubborn to make peace with her parents and she had rejected the idea vehemently—but now a cold sneaking doubt crept into her mind.

'I—I'm sorry,' she managed and meant it for Adam, for his sister and father, and underneath it all for her own family.

'Is that why you gave your brother-in-law the house—because of Nina?' Micky went on a few moments later, wanting to fill the silence when Adam still did not speak.

Adam nodded slowly. 'No doubt it'd make the old man turn in his grave if he knew—he never rewrote that spiteful will leaving everything to me, so there was no provision for Gerry and the girls when he died. But I knew that underneath all the sham and bluster he'd never stopped loving Nina, and it was only his stupid pride that had stopped him making amends when he was alive, so——'

Once more Adam lifted his shoulders in a shrug but the indifference implied by the off-hand gesture was belied by the burning intensity of conviction in his eyes.

'A damn' great house and a share in Rochford's won't make up for not having Nina, but at least it'll make sure Gerry and the kids are secure and comfortable.'

In the privacy of her own thoughts Micky was busy discarding some of her own foolish assumptions. She had never expected such honesty or, if she was truthful, such generosity and concern for others in a man she had dismissed as being solely concerned with money. She had expected Adam to be much more like his father; now she could see that he was very, very different.

Those changeable eyes were on her face, darkening suddenly until they were almost green, intent and watchful.

'Does it make you think?' he asked suddenly, a cold harsh edge to his voice.

Micky stiffened at his tone. Oh yes, it made her think all right, but her thoughts were too personal, too painful to be shared with him. Only now did she see why he had opened up to her so unexpectedly. He was trying to manipulate her once more, using the tragic example of his sister to blackmail her mentally, force her into action before she was ready. Nina's story explained some of the reasons for his concern that she should be reunited with her parents but she couldn't be sure that was his only motive.

'I——' she began then stopped, silenced by a new and very unwelcome suspicion. She had forgotten the conversation she had overheard on the night of the dinner party.

Estranged or not, she was still her father's daughter and, though her mind flinched away from the thought, she knew that ultimately she would inherit Dennison's, unless of course her father followed old John Rochford's example and cut her out of his will.

In her heart Micky knew that would never happen, her father wasn't the tyrant the older Rochford had been—but what if Adam believed it might? He had been generous with his brother-in-law but he was still a hard-headed businessman. Was it possible that in spite of everything he had hopes of consolidating the merger with Dennison's with another, more personal takeover? Her heart lurched in panic at the thought.

'My thoughts are my own, Mr Rochford,' she said stiltedly, once again using the formal title in the hope of distancing him from her.

'Mr Rochford,' Adam mimicked cynically. 'Why do you have this trouble with my name? Is Adam such a difficult thing to say? You managed it all right last night.'

Hot colour suffused Micky's cheeks. Last night she had been hurt, confused and very vulnerable, she had spoken without thinking. Still, it was crazy to stick to strict formality with someone when she had—however unwillingly—spent the night in his flat. After all, she had been thinking of him as Adam ever since those strange late-night journeys home had begun.

'Adam,' she said almost defiantly, just to prove she *could* say it, and in fact the word came easily to her tongue, there was a strange sort of pleasure in simply speaking his name.

A memory tugged at her mind and, impelled by curiosity, she demanded impetuously, 'What was it you called me last night? Not Micky—something else.'

'Midge?' Adam queried, his mouth curving in amusement. 'I thought you hadn't noticed.'

'Midge!' Micky was intrigued. 'But why?'

The curve to Adam's mouth widened into a smile.

'Midget?' he offered teasingly, the glint of humour in his eyes a clear indication that he was not telling her the real reason for the nickname. 'After all, you're only a tiny scrap of a thing.'

Micky shook her head firmly, refusing to rise to the bait.

'That's not it,' she said, thinking of long summer evenings in the garden, perfect evenings spoiled by an irritating, buzzing cloud of gnats. 'A midge is an insect, a tiny, infuriating pest that buzzes round you all the time and sometimes bites.'

Adam's grin widened even further and Micky heard the laughter deep in his throat as he leaned back in his chair.

'I think that describes you perfectly,' he said.

CHAPTER SIX

THERE were compensations to being stuck indoors with an aching knee, Micky thought as she pushed compost firmly round a geranium cutting, but unfortunately they didn't quite outweigh the disadvantages. In the past week her collection of houseplants had had more attention than ever in their lives before, and the abundance of carefully pruned, fertilised and repotted greenery that surrounded her almost made up for living in a third-floor bedsitter without access to, or even sight of, a garden. But even though her hands were busy, her mind was not and so was free to think, something she'd been doing a lot of lately—too much, because none of it got her anywhere.

With a sigh she put the geranium on the window-sill and limped to the sink to wash the dirt from her hands. They looked worse than ever these days, she thought, the ugly, bitten nails evidence of her disturbed and unhappy state of mind. Mum would throw a fit if she could see them.

Tears burned at Micky's eyes. What was her mother doing now? It was Thursday—her coffee-morning day. Impatiently she flung the towel from her, heedless of the fact that it missed the chair she had been aiming for and slid to the ground. If only she could make up her mind what to do!

For all she had refused to admit it openly, the story of Nina's estrangement from her father and its tragic ending had affected Micky strongly. She had suffered from nightmares, waking bathed in sweat at the thought that something might happen to her mother or father before the rift between them was healed, horrified by the idea that her own stubborn pride might be all that prevented that reconciliation. She missed her parents terribly. The sense of loss was like a nagging ache, always with her, even in the first heady weeks she had spent with Zac.

Zac! Micky brought her hand down hard on the draining-board, letting the physical pain distract her from the bitterness in her mind. Headstrong, devil-may-care, volatile Zac; she had given him her heart and her body, built her dreams around him, and in two short months he had totally devastated her.

The early weeks had been a whirlwind of sensation, a whole new sense of freedom and a reckless indifference to the future. For perhaps fifty days she had shared Zac's life, his flat, his bed in the belief that she was the centre of his world as he was of hers, so that nothing else mattered. If there had been a flaw in her contentment it had been the result of her own nervousness when they made love. Ignorance and inexperience made her awkward, tensed muscles that should have been languid and relaxed, closed her mouth against Zac's passionate kisses and had her murmuring embarrassed excuses.

She had believed that all she needed was time, time to learn how to relax and how to show her love in a physical way, but Zac had been openly impatient of her nervousness, regarding a sexual relationship as a natural progression from holding hands, and night after night Micky had lain awake, feeling empty and restless, knowing deep in her heart that something vital was missing, that there had to be more to lovemaking than this.

She must have been blind and deaf because she hadn't seen it coming. She had known of Zac's reputation as a womaniser; living in the flat with his friends, it had been impossible not to notice how often girls' names had come up in the conversation accompanied by a sly glance and a knowing smile, but she had foolishly believed that his feelings for her were different. So it had hit her with the force of a nuclear explosion, tearing her apart, when, on New Year's Day, after an uncomfortable week of rows and accusations that she was cold and unresponsive, Zac had announced that he found no satisfaction in making love to a woman who knew damn' all about pleasing a man and she had better start looking for somewhere else to live.

The tears that had threatened earlier had vanished now, leaving Micky's eyes achingly dry. There had been tears enough over Zac in those first few days when she had thought she would never stop crying, weeping out the pain and disillusionment, the sense of betrayal not only by Zac but also by herself. She had been living out a delusion, seeing only what she wanted to. In her foolish love she had rushed in blindly, dashing headlong into a relationship that had no roots, no foundation, only the transient impulses of the moment, and as a result she had betrayed her own deepest needs and feelings, realising exactly what she had lost only when it was far, far too late.

Two sharp blasts on a car horn in the street jolted Micky from her unhappy reverie, sending her thoughts into other, equally unsettling channels. She couldn't face Adam now, she didn't feel up to coping with any company, least of all his, for Adam was another problem she couldn't come to terms with.

But she had no chance of avoiding him. He would know she couldn't be out. He had been at her flat only the night before and knew how far her leg was from being fully healed. He had called every night this week and had taken to sounding his horn as he parked his car to warn her of his arrival, so that she had time to make her way to the door slowly and carefully with as little discomfort as possible.

She'd left it a little too late as it was. Adam was already mounting the last flight of stairs as she opened the door, and an unreasoning resentment flared as she compared the ease with which he took two steps at a time with her own ungainly hobble. As a result her response to his cheerful greeting was gruff and ungracious, earning her a drily reproving, 'Now, is that any way to greet me when I've come here as an angel of mercy to rescue you from your imprisonment?'

In spite of herself, Micky couldn't suppress a swift spurt of laughter, unable to imagine Adam as anything remotely like an angel. But then an image sprang from nowhere into her mind. In an illustrated Bible she had had as a child there had been a picture of the Archangel Michael, and his face had had the same powerful beauty that stamped Adam's features; a strong, masculine beauty with nothing soft or feminine about it.

And he *had* been an angel of mercy during the past week. He had visited her every day, bringing books, magazines, fruit—but never flowers. Clearly he remembered her provocative comments on the bouquet he had given her mother. The gifts were dropped casually on to the table with a 'take them or leave them' gesture and never referred to again, but it was impossible not to notice that he had taken time and trouble to choose things she would like, using clues he had gleaned from their conversation the night before—like the time they had discovered a mutual passion for science fiction. That had resulted in a bundle of books she had always meant to read but had never had the time to.

At first their conversation had been stilted and awkward, Micky's responses to Adam's questions being carefully reticent, but he had patiently drawn her out, asking just the right sort of questions to loosen her tongue without making her feel that he was prying into things that she didn't want him to know. He had answered her own few tentative queries about himself with the same direct honesty that he had shown when he had told her about Nina and in his admission of the way he had failed his exams.

Micky had appreciated that honesty, and after seven days of his casual friendliness she had come to look forward to his visits, in spite of the way they made her feel uncomfortable at the suspicion that perhaps she had once again jumped to conclusions just as he had accused her of doing. He had certainly shown no sign of any amorous inclinations. There had been at least two occasions when she had gone to the door to see him out and he had paused to look deep into her face, almost as if he might kiss her. But instead he had simply touched her cheek in a light, impersonal gesture rather like that of a brother to a much younger sister and then gone without a word, leaving Micky to go back into the flat feeling confused and disturbed by the restless, dissatisfied mood that had taken hold of her.

But this visit was clearly different. For one thing, never before had Adam called so early in the day. He rarely left his office before six—and what was that he had said about release from imprisonment? Adam smiled as Micky framed the question.

'You must be going crazy shut up here like this. It's time you got out a bit.'

'But my leg——' Micky began but Adam brushed aside her protest with an imperious gesture.

'If you can make it downstairs I'll provide the transport. I was supposed to be entertaining a client tonight but the wretched man cried off at the last minute, so I'm left with a table booked and no one to share it with me. It seemed a pity to waste it so I thought of you. How about it?'

It was very cleverly done. The invitation had been given in much the same way as he had offered those other gifts, with just the right degree of carelessness; not so indifferent as to be positively insulting, but casual enough to imply no strings. Anything else would have had her muttering an immediate refusal—so why did she feel disappointed that there had been nothing more? Micky shook herself mentally. What was happening to her? She seemed incapable of seeing anything straight anymore.

'Well, do you want to come?'

Did she? The answer was there, ready-formed, before she really had time to think.

'Yes, please—I'd love to.'

What harm would it do anyway? she rationalised as she stood at the door listening to the sound of Adam's footsteps descending the stairs. He was right, she was going crazy imprisoned in those four walls. Another night spent staring at the dowdy blue roses on the wallpaper and she felt she would scream.

She needed company too. Susie had been virtually non-existent over the past week; totally involved with the new love of her life, she hadn't even been home for two nights and it seemed a long, long time since Micky herself had had an evening out. Working at Garbo's did nothing for her social life, and since the break-up with Zac she had avoided all her old haunts, afraid of seeing him with the girl who had replaced her—or, more likely the one after that; her two months with Zac had been something of a record.

Just once she had ventured out to the disco—with disastrous results. Micky shuddered at the memory. Zac hadn't been there but Tony, one of his flatmates, had seen her. She had been glad of his company at first but later, when he had walked her home, the evening had turned into a nightmare. Tony's crude taunts were etched into her mind; if she closed her eyes she could still see his contemptuously leering face and since then she had refused any offers of a date from anyone.

But Adam wasn't offering her a 'date'. He had an empty evening to fill, a table booked, and he knew she needed company. He was, in his own words, being an angel of mercy in rescuing her from her loneliness, and she could accept that gesture gratefully because it was all she wanted—or at least that was what she told herself, but try as she might she couldn't quite suppress the dull ache of regret that it was nothing more.

She should have known! Micky's heart sank right to the soles of her red canvas boots as Adam parked the car outside the restaurant that evening. After all, he had said he had originally been planning to entertain a client, so she supposed she should have expected something like this imposing, exclusive establishment that drained her confidence as soon as she saw it, adding to the awkwardness imposed on her by her stiff and aching knee as Adam helped her out of the car.

His hand lingered on her arm, steadying her as she tried to avoid putting her full weight on her leg. It was improving, the swelling had gone down and the bruises had faded, but it would be some days yet before she would be able to move with any real ease. She had needed Adam's support to get downstairs from her bedsitter and now she was intensely grateful when, without a word, he tucked her hand under his arm so that she could lean on him as they headed towards the brightly lit restaurant.

Micky felt the strength of taut muscle beneath the fine, supple leather of Adam's jacket and breathed a silent prayer of thankfulness for its support—but then as they reached the main door and his arm came round her waist to help her up the steps, the purely practical need for his assistance vanished, swamped by a tidal wave of heightened physical sensation.

On Adam's part the move was just an automatic gesture of courtesy, but the effect on Micky was like a burning electric current shooting through every nerve. The slight movement had drawn her nearer to Adam's lean, hard body. She could feel the warmth of his skin through the fine material of his shirt, scent the tangy aftershave she remembered clinging to his jacket on the night of her fall, but now it was mixed with the clean, male scent of Adam himself, and the sudden searing heat that suffused her veins made her stand still in shock, her head reeling and her eyes going to Adam's face as if to try to read there just what had happened.

It all took perhaps ten seconds, and though to Adam it must simply have appeared that she had paused to draw breath and gather her strength for the final flight of steps, to Micky it seemed as if time had suddenly stopped, hung suspended, and then jolted back into action again. When she continued on up the steps she felt strangely unreal, insubstantial and dreamlike. It was as if a whirlwind had suddenly swept her from the path of life she had thought she was destined to follow, spun her high in the air and dropped her down again on a totally new and unknown route; one without signposts or any landmark she recognised, so that she crossed the restaurant in a daze and sank weakly into the chair Adam pulled out for her, feeling that her legs wouldn't support her a moment longer.

'Midge?' Adam's voice was sharp with concern and his hand touched her shoulder gently. 'What is it? You're quite white.'

'I'll be all right.' It came out in a quavering, shaky gasp. She wished he would move away, his closeness was doing alarming things to her pulse-rate and his touch, light as it was, seemed to burn through the satin blouse, scorching her skin. 'Just give me a minute,' she pleaded.

To her relief Adam moved away, but even when he seated himself opposite her Micky felt no better. If anything she felt worse, supremely conscious of the intensity of that searching gaze on her face.

'I—my leg is more painful than I'd realised,' she managed, dragging the most plausible excuse she could from the recesses of her mind. 'Getting here shook me up a bit.'

As her breathing steadied she risked a glance at Adam's face and immediately wished she hadn't. It was like looking at a completely different man—not a stranger—those strong features and clear hazel eyes were so familiar, and yet no longer the same. She had thought him attractive before but never with the intensity with which she felt it now.

Now there was no room for anything in her mind beyond the potently sexual magnetism of the man before her. It hit her with the force of a blow to her stomach, driving the breath from her body and leaving her weak and shaking. It was nothing like the immediate attraction she had felt for Zac; it had crept up on her slowly and insidiously and she had been unaware of its progress until it had exploded in her face in that moment outside.

Using her menu as a shield from Adam's eyes, Micky forced her attention on to it, trying to regain some sort of control, but the print blurred and swam before her eyes. If only she could go back, still see Adam as the much older, sleekly groomed man she had first met! But that man had gone for good. She couldn't find a trace of him in the Adam who sat opposite her, his burnished copper hair gleaming in the light of the lamps, his broad chest and shoulders emphasised by the soft leather jacket that clung like a second skin. One long, strong-looking hand lay on the table-top, just inches away from Micky's, and the temptation to reach out and lay her own hand over it, just to touch him, was overwhelming. She had even lifted her hand ever so slightly—then froze as Adam spoke.

'Well? Made up your mind?'

'I'm not——' Micky's throat felt dry and her voice sounded rough and hoarse. 'I'm not really very hungry.' And that was the truth. In that shocking moment of realisation her appetite had completely deserted her. 'Well, just steak and salad then,' she added in a hasty response to Adam's frown, knowing very well that, whatever she ordered, she wouldn't even taste it.

To her intense relief the waiter arrived then, distracting Adam's attention and giving Micky a few much-needed minutes to collect her thoughts. Wanting to look anywhere but at Adam until she was calmer, she glanced around the room, catching one or two frankly curious stares cast in their direction by other diners.

This was not exactly surprising, she admitted ruefully. They must look an ill-matched pair to say the least—Adam, elegant and self-assured in his understatedly stylish clothes, and herself—Micky banged her glass down with unnecessary force, the doubts that had assailed her in the moment she had seen the restaurant resurfacing with a vengeance.

'What the hell's the matter now?' Adam demanded, every trace of concern gone from his voice and replaced by a hard, impatient note.

'People are staring,' Micky muttered gruffly, snatching at the smallest of her worries as the least dangerous to mention.

'So why should that worry you?' he responded drily. 'I thought the whole point of dressing as you do was to make people notice you.'

And of course there was no way she could refute that. In the past she *had* wanted to stand out, or at least appear different. Just a few short months ago she wouldn't have cared if the whole world had stared—so why did it matter now? Because it did matter; subconsciously she had known that when she was getting ready this evening.

She had tried on almost every item in her wardrobe and nothing had seemed right. Suddenly clothes that seemed fun, if a little outrageous, had appeared garish, tasteless, and downright ugly. She couldn't imagine what had possessed her to buy them, and the realisation that most if not all of them had been bought solely to impress Zac had only added to her dislike of the offending items. In the end she had chosen a crimson satin blouse with a peplum waist and a narrow black leather skirt. In the privacy of her room they hadn't looked too bad, but now she felt they must appear loud and tarty.

And of course it was too late to wish she had stuck to her original decision to tone down her make-up too. At first she had experimented with just a smoky blue eyeshadow that picked up the colour of her eyes, but, finding that made her look little more than fourteen, she had added a second, silver-grey eyeshadow, eyeliner, and a thick coating of mascara on her long, curling lashes. She could do nothing about her hair, neither the style nor the colour of it, and the soft, freshly washed strands of her over-long fringe fell forward, irritatingly, into her eyes so that she felt she must look like a small, uncertain Yorkshire terrier.

'Actually you look quite presentable,' Adam surprised her by saying, then spoiled the effect by adding, 'for you, that is. I'd expected gold lamé and green tights, or perhaps a leather motorbike jacket covered in studs like Mr Hamer's.'

Micky scowled at the taunt and the mention of Zac. It was the first time his name had come up between them since the meeting in the coffee bar. In fact, Adam had been so reticent on the subject that she had begun to wonder if he knew what had happened and was being carefully tactful. It was perfectly possible that he did; he seemed to know everything else about her. All the same, it was time she cleared the air in the matter once and for all.

'I don't see Zac any more,' she declared defiantly.

'I know.'

Well, she'd expected that, but it took the wind out of her sails all the same, forcing her to wonder once again just how much he knew about her relationship with Zac. He had said nothing that even hinted at condemnation or disapproval of her actions where Zac was concerned, which, remembering the impossibly high standards he was reputed to have where women were concerned, was what she might have expected from him. So was his silence the result of ignorance rather than tact? It was an uncomfortable speculation and one which was made all the worse by the fact that both interpretations were equally destructive to her peace of mind.

'What don't you know?' she snapped to hide her discomposure. 'Have you had me followed or what? Tell me, did you hire a private detective to track me down or did you do your own snooping?'

Adam sighed exaggeratedly, leaning back in his chair and folding his arms, his eyes on her face, noting the way it had hardened, the bitter expression draining all the youth from her small face, making it look years older.

'I knew it was too good to last,' he murmured ironically.

'What——?' Micky began but was interrupted by the return of the waiter with the wine-list.

She watched with ill-concealed impatience as Adam, deliberately it seemed, indulged in an unnecessarily lengthy discussion before finally making his selection. As soon as they were alone again, irritated by his delaying tactics, she launched into angry speech.

'And just what was that remark supposed to mean?'

A slow smile curled Adam's lips, drawing Micky's eyes to his mouth as irresistibly as a needle is drawn to a magnet. She didn't want to feel like this! She couldn't handle it! But all the same there was a very sensual pleasure in just letting her eyes linger on that firm, beautifully shaped mouth, in just *thinking* of what it would be like to feel those lips on hers. The realisation of the direction in which her thoughts were heading brought Micky's head up sharply, making her eyes wide and apprehensive as Adam leaned forward again to answer her.

'For the last week you've treated me as if I was something like a human being. Just for a while you'd forgotten that, in your mind at least, I was supposed to be the villain in all this. Now suddenly I'm the big bad wolf all over again.'

Adam's tone was quiet, but there was a cold light in the eyes that were fixed on her face, one that sent a sensation like the trickle of icy water down Micky's spine. He was right, she had forgotten—or at least put to one side—the fact that it was partly because of Adam that she was alienated from her parents. At first he had deliberately kept them apart—but now he seemed determined to achieve exactly the opposite, and she didn't really know why. His words had made her take a step back from the situation and see how dangerously close she had come to trusting him without any proof that he did not have some ulterior motive for his behaviour so that her anger was mixed with a bitter sense of loss as she answered him.

'Well, what did you expect?' she demanded, her voice high and brittle. 'If you set out to manipulate others, run their lives, you can't expect them to like it!'

'Is that what you think I'm trying to do—manipulate you?' The question came with a deceptive mildness.

'Well, aren't you?' Once again Micky had that feeling of having her back against the wall, as if pinned there by the intensity of those cold, eagle's eyes. 'You've been interfering ever since the day you first came to the house, maybe even before then. You were the one who encouraged Dad to let me go in the first place, without you he'd never have done that.'

Adam's slight nod of agreement was expected and infuriating. Incensed by his calm admission of the way he had influenced her father against her, Micky continued angrily, 'Then, on your own admission, *you* told Mum and Dad not to contact me, you hunted me down—and you've been hounding me ever since, harassing me non-stop.'

The sardonically questioning lift to one eyebrow almost defeated her. She knew she was only telling half the truth. The memory of his gentleness on the night of her accident, his kindness since, slid into her mind like a reproach, but she forced it away again. It altered nothing of the rest of the situation.

'And now for some reason you're determined I should go back home because—God knows why!—you've decided its what *you* want. Who—or what—gives you the right to bully me like this!'

'Am I bullying you?'

Once again the question came in that quiet, almost gentle voice, making Micky shake her head confusedly. She didn't know how to handle this coolly impassive Adam. He had never really *bullied* her, and just lately he had changed his tactics, eased off on any sort of pressure—and yet she still felt threatened. The disturbing thought that it might be her own conscience that made her feel like this made her shake her head again to clear her mind.

'Does that mean no, I'm not bullying you or no, you won't answer my question?' Adam demanded, his tone sharpening noticeably.

'You're bullying me now!' Micky countered defensively.

'And you're avoiding the issue,' Adam flashed back. His long fingers drummed on the table-top in a restless, angry movement, then he stilled them suddenly, his eyes as light and cold as ice. 'I think it's about time we did some straight talking, young lady. From where I stand we appear to have two alternatives—you can stop running, face up to the fact that you're not a child any more but an adult and that means taking responsibility for your own actions. You can explain to me exactly what it is you're kicking against and why—or you can retreat into your adolescent rebellion in which case we forget the whole damn' thing! If you play straight with me, I'll do the same for you—but I warn you, Micky, if you chicken out this time I'll take you back to that revolting bedsitter and leave you there and forget you ever existed! So tell me, which is it to be?'

CHAPTER SEVEN

'OKAY, Micky, I want a decision.'

Micky shivered at the steely note in Adam's voice. The few minutes' grace the arrival of their meal had given her had not been enough for her to collect her thoughts and put them in any sort of order. Her stomach twisted nervously as she saw the stony, implacable set to Adam's face—and those eyes! How could she ever have thought them warm or friendly?

Earlier she had wanted to be able to look at him and see only the arrogant, domineering devil of a man she had convinced herself she hated but now, seeing him with the veneer of friendliness stripped away, faced once more with the hard, purposeful creature who had been the bane of her life ever since he had come into it, she knew that it changed nothing.

Adam had threatened to forget that she ever existed and she believed him to be more than capable of carrying out that threat, and the pain that admission brought told her that *she* could never forget *him*. He had turned her world upside down, made her question, made her doubt herself, but in spite of that she wouldn't trade the earlier days when everything had seemed so much less complicated for the uncertainty she felt now.

'Micky!' Adam prompted warningly and the harshness in his voice closed her throat so that once more she could only shake her head despairingly, not knowing how or where to begin.

To her horror, clearly interpreting the gesture as one of refusal, Adam flung his napkin on the table and pushed back his chair. Terror that he might actually carry out his threat and take her home jolted Micky into speech.

'No!' she gasped. 'Adam, please—I want to talk!'

For one dreadful moment she thought she had left it too late but then Adam slowly subsided into his chair again.

'Go on,' he commanded coldly.

Micky swallowed hard, hunting for the right words. 'I don't think you understand . . .'

Her voice died as she heard what she was saying. You don't understand, the age-old cry of the adolescent hitting out against the inevitability of having to grow up. Was that what she had been doing? Had she ever really *thought* about her actions?

Every trace of colour left Micky's cheeks and her hand crept up over her mouth as if to block any further speech as she stared at Adam, numb with the shock of the revelation. She saw his eyes narrow swiftly as he watched the swift succession of emotions, shock, fear, realisation and shame, that crossed her face and he waited silently until she took a long, tremulous breath. Then he leaned forward, intent hazel eyes locking with wide, uncertain blue ones.

'Try me,' he said softly.

It was hard, in fact it was hell, because each time she tried to give him her side of things she saw the other. Her new-found understanding shone like a spotlight on her memories, lighting up things that had been hidden until now, pushing into shadow things she had always considered important, until in the end she gave up trying to review and revise as she went along and simply gave Adam the facts without interpretation.

As she spoke, Micky relived those times of change and upheaval, the alienation from her parents as they became absorbed in new concerns, the loss of contact with old friends, the move to the new house, new school. It was there that she had first started dressing outrageously, she recalled. Out of her depth and floundering, unable to match the casual chic of her schoolmates, she had rebelled against it. The more the girls had laughed, the more her parents had objected, the more determined she had become. Then she had met a group of former pupils of her old school, people who made her feel she wasn't so very different after all. She had spent all her free time with them—and it was through them that she had met Zac.

Her voice faltered, lost any trace of conviction, when she tried to revive the hostility she had felt at her parents' disapproval of Zac. Sadder and wiser now, she saw their opposition not as the snobbishness she had believed it to be but as the natural concern of caring parents who had distrusted Zac's motives. If only she had listened to them instead of following her own headstrong course—a path that had led to bitter humiliation and unhappiness.

'Is that it?' Adam asked as the flow of words ground to a halt and Micky sank back in her chair. She felt drained and exhausted but somehow better—cleaner, as if the whole process had been an exorcism of the past. 'Have you told me everything?'

Micky avoided those probing eyes as she nodded silently. She had told him almost everything—everything he needed to know, anyway. But there was one private memory she had not exorcised, one raw, unhealed wound that she couldn't let him see. She could visualise in her mind Zac's bored, indifferent expression as he declared to her face that 'this thing between them' had burned itself out, the impatience with which he had dismissed her ardent declarations of love, and somehow the image, rather than fading with time, now seemed suddenly sharper and clearer in a new and infinitely more painful way. It wasn't only the memory that hurt but the fear of how Adam might react to it that twisted something savagely deep inside her.

Because something had happened in that moment when Adam had looked her straight in the eye and said, 'Try me,' in that quiet, encouraging voice. She had known then that she didn't hate him any more; perhaps she had never hated him. What she *did* feel was too new and too fragile to define but it was there, like some tiny seedling nestling snugly in the dark earth, needing only a touch of the sun to make it grow. If she told Adam everything then perhaps there would be no sun. His face might fill with disgust as Zac's had done, and if he turned away the precious seed would wither and die.

Adam had sat silently through her outpourings, listening hard and only occasionally putting in some question if she hesitated, but now he rested his clasped hands on the table, directing the full force of those clear eyes on her face in a way that held Micky mesmerised.

'You've had your say,' he told her quietly. 'Now it's your turn to listen.' And with a shiver of apprehension Micky recognised that the truce was over and he was returning to the attack.

But strangely enough she didn't mind; in fact she almost welcomed it, because in that moment of revelation she had realised just why she had felt afraid and trapped and hostile towards Adam. She *had* been running away, too scared to face the truth that she was every bit as much to blame for her problems as her parents. So she listened, no longer thinking his words cruel and hateful but honest and essential if she was to recognise the truth.

What Adam said would hurt; it was bound to. You couldn't cut away the dead wood of years of delusion and prejudice without pain, but it was a constructive pain. Just as it was vital to prune back a rose bush to encourage new and healthy growth in the future, so now it was important that she hurt for a while so as to come out all the stronger in the end.

'Your father is a fine man, Micky,' Adam was saying, undisguised sincerity ringing in his voice. 'He took on a hard job with Dennison's—that place was heading for bankruptcy when he inherited it and he's done a damn' good job of getting it back into shape—which is all the more admirable when you consider that he was way out of his depth at the beginning. So he's been obsessed with the place—' Micky winced as Adam quoted her own words back at her '—but he's *had* to be. He's been learning, fighting, and if he'd let his concentration slip for a minute Dennison's would have been in the hands of the receivers within six months, and that would have meant the loss of God knows how many jobs. Your father knows what it's like to be unemployed—he had twelve months on the dole when you were a baby and he was determined it wouldn't happen to his employees if he could prevent it. You didn't know that, did you?' Adam added sharply, seeing the look on Micky's face.

Micky shook her head slowly. She had been vaguely aware of the fact that her parents had had some hard times in the past, but she had never really known the details. It was an uncomfortable and shaming feeling to realise that this man knew her own mother and father better than she did herself.

'They never talked to me about things like that,' she said hesitantly, and Adam sighed faintly.

'No, they didn't—and that's part of the problem. You told me yourself you were a delicate baby and you're your parents' only child so they spoilt you, tried to protect you for as long as they could. I think you'll find they know it was a mistake now, but it was done with the best possible motives. They wanted to give you the best in life, all the advantages they never had, and when Dennison's came along it meant that they could give you more than they'd ever dreamed of—money, security, education.'

'But they didn't ask what I wanted! They didn't talk to me!' Micky couldn't help saying.

'And did you talk to them?' Adam shot back. 'You argued, you shouted, you defied them every inch of the way—but did you ever really *talk*?'

He read the answer in Micky's white face without her having to speak and his eyes darkened suddenly.

'For God's sake, Micky—when families stop talking they die!'

Micky's breath caught in her throat at the sudden naked emotion in his voice. Those clear eyes were shadowed, clouded by the memory of the way his own family had been torn apart, and her heart twisted in sympathy. Adam himself must have been torn in two, she thought, his love for his sister and his father, each in conflict with his loyalty to the other. Suddenly her own quarrel with her parents seemed petty and childish.

Adam was watching her, his gaze disturbingly direct.

'You've stopped fighting me, Midge,' he murmured softly.

Micky coloured faintly under his scrutiny, unaware of the way the flush of colour drove the last of the bitterness from her face leaving her looking very young and infinitely vulnerable. He had called her Midge, she thought, her heart lifting so that the eyes she turned on Adam glowed warmly.

'I don't think I want to fight you any more,' she whispered, her voice trembling on the words.

She had meant to go on but a sudden change in Adam's face, a tiny, involuntary movement of his hand towards her, froze the words on her lips. For a long silent moment their eyes locked together, the tension between them almost tangible, a tension that was mirrored in the tautness of the muscles of Adam's shoulders under the smooth fit of his jacket, and when he finally broke the spell that held them by reaching abruptly for his wine-glass Micky found that her muscles too ached from the strain of being held unnaturally stiffly.

For the first time since she had met him Adam seemed ill at ease and unsure of what to say as he swirled his wine around his glass, staring down at it and frowning very slightly. The sight of his discomposure was so novel to Micky that she studied him unreservedly, intrigued by the sudden change in him and at a loss to discover what had brought it about. The strange uncertainty changed him, softening his expression, bringing a new vulnerability to the hard, strong face, giving it a younger, almost boyish appearance, an impression that was enhanced by the way his chestnut hair had escaped its sleek confinement and fallen forwards over his face.

Just what had that look meant? She had thought she was coming to know Adam, but it seemed he had an infinite ability to surprise her. Micky coloured uncontrollably at the recollection of how Adam had accused her of having him catalogued, filed and indexed before she had even talked to him, and the thought made her shift uncomfortably in her seat.

The slight movement brought Adam out of his sudden abstraction. The faintest hint of that unfathomable expression still lingered in his eyes but as Micky watched it flickered like a candle flame and went out and he slipped back into casual conversation as if the moment had never been.

'Did you get that job problem sorted out?' he asked and Micky wrinkled her nose in distaste.

'Danny says he'll keep my place until Monday and no longer.' She'd almost told him not to bother, she remembered. After a week away from Garbo's she'd come to realise how much she hated the place and her job; it wasn't the sort of thing she wanted to do at all. When Adam spoke again it was almost as if he had read her mind.

'If your father hadn't inherited Dennison's, what would you really have wanted to do?'

Micky's eyes slid to her plate, her face a picture of embarrassment. 'You'll laugh,' she muttered awkwardly.

'Why?' Adam sounded intrigued. 'Is it such a crazy ambition?'

'No.' It wasn't crazy at all, but no one had taken her seriously when she had said what she wanted to do—and her mother had been frankly incredulous.

'So tell me,' Adam insisted.

'I wanted to be a gardener.' It came out defensively and Micky's head came up at the sound Adam made in his throat. His eyes looked suspiciously bright. 'I knew you'd laugh!' she accused him angrily.

'I'm not laughing, Midge—at least not at that,' Adam told her seriously. 'I was just thinking how you always manage to surprise me—and I was thinking of the flowers.'

'Flowers?' Micky echoed, wondering what he meant by his first remark—and just how she had surprised him before. 'You mean the ones you brought for Mum?'

Adam nodded, a smile lighting his face. 'And you laid into me for not leaving them to grow naturally.'

'You gave as good as you got!' Micky retorted lightly, slanting a teasing, mischievous glance at his face. 'And I didn't mean it really. I was a bit jealous, no one ever brought me flowers.'

'I'll have to remember that.' At least that was what Micky thought Adam said, but his voice was so low she might have misheard him completely. 'But I don't understand,' he went on more clearly, 'you had a magnificent garden at home so why didn't you——?'

Adam stopped suddenly as the smile faded from Micky's face, leaving her looking lost and forlorn.

'We had a gardener to look after that. I wasn't supposed to help. You see, Mum hated the mess gardening made of my hands. She wanted me to behave like a lady, look like a lady. I'm afraid she didn't succeed.'

Impulsively Micky pulled her hands from under the table and held them out towards Adam, the broken nails openly displayed.

'See?' Her smile was rueful. 'These aren't a lady's hands.'

It was then that Adam did a surprising thing, something that made Micky's heart jerk unevenly, increasing her pulse-rate dramatically. He reached out and took her hands in both of his, holding them gently but firmly, his touch warm and strong. His thumbs smoothed the skin on the insides of her wrists with a movement that was hypnotically soothing but at the same time sent a quiver of excitement running up her arm.

'Not in the way your mother meant, perhaps,' he said slowly, his eyes fixed on her upturned palms. 'But——'

But the words he would have said were never spoken for at that moment a woman's laughter rang out across the restaurant and Adam's head jerked up at the sound, his eyes going to the doorway. Following the direction of his gaze, Micky felt a sharp, stabbing sensation flash through her as she saw the tall, elegant woman who had just come in. There was a lady, she thought bitterly—in her mother's or anyone else's sense of the word; a lady from the top of that smooth blonde head to the toes of her smart snakeskin shoes—and a very beautiful, glamorous lady at that! And to judge from the way Adam was staring at her, he thought so too.

'Someone you know?' she asked, disturbed by the jerky, breathless way her words came out and by the sudden emptiness she felt as Adam abruptly let her hands drop back on to the table.

'Someone I knew,' he corrected curtly, pushing back his chair with a brusque movement. 'I think it's time we left,' he went on, getting to his feet.

'But——' Micky tried to protest but Adam was already moving across the room, leaving her with no alternative but to limp awkwardly after him.

It was as Adam paused to pay the bill that the blonde woman noticed them. Micky saw her eyes rest on Adam, widening slightly in recognition, then she detached herself from the group she was with and glided towards them.

'Adam darling, how wonderful to see you.' The low voice was soft and caressing as the woman laid a hand on Adam's arm to gain his attention—an elegantly manicured hand of course, Micky noted bitterly, the perfection of those carefully painted nails making her push her own hands deep into the pockets of her skirt.

'Lauren.' Adam's acknowledgement of the greeting was brief to the point of rudeness.

Lauren? Not Julie then, or Miranda, or any of the names she heard connected with Adam's, and if that curt greeting was anything to go by, *not* someone he even liked. The sudden lifting of her spirits at that thought rocked Micky's sense of reality, sending her into a daze of confusion from which she surfaced only when she caught a phrase that clearly referred to herself.

'Aren't you going to introduce me to your little friend?' Lauren asked, and Micky thought she detected a malicious humour in the emphasis on 'little', so that she drew herself up stiffly, her temper threatening to get the better of her. This Lauren might look a lady on the surface, but underneath it all she was a grade-one bitch!—There she went again, she caught herself up reprovingly—jumping to conclusions.

But her resolve not to judge so hastily was completely destroyed when the blonde woman added in a whisper that was carefully pitched so as to reach Micky's ears, 'Really, Adam, she's only a child! Have you taken to cradle-snatching?'

'I leave that sort of thing to you,' Adam returned smoothly, but with enough bite in his voice to distract Micky from her own muddled feelings and glance sharply at his face. There were undercurrents here that she didn't understand. 'Micky's just the daughter of a very good friend,' Adam continued. 'Now, if you'll excuse us——'

To Micky's utter consternation he slid an arm around her waist, drawing her with him towards the door. Too stunned to think, she moved as if in a dream, conscious of the other woman's eyes following them until they were out of sight. Even then, Adam did not remove his arm, but kept it round her all the time as they crossed the courtyard towards the car but by then Micky was in no fit state to notice. In fact she needed Adam's support far more than she had done when they arrived—and this time her bruised knee had nothing to do with the weakness she felt.

If her leg hurt she didn't notice it. Her body put one foot in front of the other automatically but her mind was totally divorced from her actions. In the mass of whirling, confused thoughts two things stood out. One was the intense pleasure she felt at simply having Adam's arm around her, the light but firm pressure of his hand at her waist a heady delight that affected her far more than any of the wine she had drunk with her meal. She felt so right, so complete, held close to him like this, but mixed with that feeling was a bitter, sour sensation that tainted her happiness. Adam's careless, 'Just the daughter of a very good friend' burned in her mind like acid, leaving a raw, painful wound, because only when he had said those words had she realised that she wanted to be much, much more to him than that.

Not a word passed between them until they were once more seated in the car. Then at last Adam turned to her, his face shadowed and unreadable in the darkened interior.

'Micky,' he began and the word jolted Micky from her daze. She had no idea why he had once more abandoned his personal nickname for her, but she didn't like the change. It seemed to reinforce the way he had described her to Lauren, and her newly-heightened sensitivity to that brought her swinging round to him.

'Did you have to rush me away like that?' she demanded, hiding the hurt behind an assumed anger. 'I was enjoying myself!'

'I didn't want to stay!' Adam snapped, slamming his fist down on the steering-wheel with a violence that had Micky shrinking away from him. At once his expression changed, the smouldering anger dying from his eyes as his fist unclenched. 'I'm sorry,' he went on more quietly. 'But I wanted to get you out of there fast. I didn't want Lauren to get her claws into you. Believe me, she eats babies like you for breakfast.'

Babies! Micky wanted to scream the word out loud to ease the pain she felt at his words. To Adam she was still just a child, Bill Dennison's young daughter, nothing more. It was unbearable, coming so soon after that moment on their arrival at the restaurant when she had first realised the full force of the attraction Adam held for her. She hadn't felt like a child then; she had felt all woman. Dimly she became aware that Adam was speaking again.

'There was another reason, too,' he was saying. 'I said I wanted to talk to you and I still do—but I have no intention of holding a personal conversation in a public restaurant with Lauren and her cronies only feet away. So if I ask you to come back to my flat will you come—or will you start fighting me again?'

Micky struggled to pinpoint exactly what it was that was different about Adam's voice. It was strangely hesitant, almost diffident, as if he was unsure of her reaction. It reminded her of that moment of uncertainty he had shown earlier, reviving the confusion she had felt at his reaction. But in spite of her bewilderment she knew there was only one answer she could give because, as she had already told him, she no longer wanted to fight him.

CHAPTER EIGHT

'MAKE yourself at home,' Adam instructed as he and Micky entered the welcoming living-room of his flat. He shrugged himself out of his jacket and flung it carelessly over the back of the settee as he added, 'I'll fix us both a drink—*not* brandy?'

'Not brandy,' Micky confirmed with a smile at yet another of those small indications of the trouble he took to remember her likes and dislikes—not that it made her anything special, she told herself with painful honesty. The courtesy was so instinctive, he probably did for everyone. 'I'll stick to wine,' she added hastily to cover the pang of regret.

While Adam was busy with the drinks, Micky flicked idly through the large collection of records that were stored under an elaborate music centre on the opposite side of the room, scarcely noticing what she was doing because her mind was on other things, as she reflected on the difference between this visit and the last time she had been in Adam's flat. The Micky of that night seemed like a stranger to her, in fact she had the uncomfortable feeling that she didn't like her former self very much at all. From now on things were going to be different, she resolved. She would learn from her mistakes, and perhaps then she could make up for the mess she had made of things in the past. Her hand stilled on the records as she spotted a familiar title.

'Billy Joel!' she exclaimed in surprise and delight at discovering one of her own favourites.

Perhaps there was rather more surprise in her voice than she had intended, certainly Adam seemed to interpret it that way as his mouth twisted a trifle cynically.

'I didn't exactly come out of the ark,' he murmured, the dry irony of his tone catching Micky off balance so that, without thinking, she blurted out the question that had been fretting at her mind ever since the first time she had met him.

'How old *are* you?'

'I shall be thirty at the end of July,' Adam stated frankly then he frowned at the expression on her face. 'And just what is that busy little mind of yours going to make of that?' he enquired sardonically. 'Thirty years old—I must seem well over the hill to you.'

'Oh, no!' That wasn't what she had been thinking at all. What had really been in her mind was the crazy idea that he seemed to grow younger, the age gap between them lessening every time she met him. Micky's confusion increased as she realised that she had spoken her thoughts out loud.

Adam's laugh was one of genuine amusement, a rich, warm sound that touched something deep in Micky's heart, sending a glow of happiness through her veins.

'A biological impossibility—but flattering all the same,' he commented with the smile that had set her heart pounding before—as it did now. 'Put one of those on if you like,' he added with a nod in the direction of the records.

'I'd love to!' Micky did not try to hide her enthusiasm. 'I left all my records at home, and Zac——'

Strangely, it was as if Adam hadn't noticed the way Micky's words had been choked off. Without a word he handed her a glass then strolled over to the record collection, selected one and placed it on the turntable. Only when the music flowed out into the room did he turn and give her a long, considering look.

'So tell me about Zac,' he said casually.

No! Micky thought. He was getting too close, probing too deep into memories she hadn't come to terms with. Susie had laughed at her fears, declaring that no one gave a damn about virginity any more, but

Micky found it impossible to forget those exacting standards Adam was reputed to have and she knew she had to put him off.

'Zac hated Billy Joel's songs,' she offered lamely. It *was* what she had meant to say but it wasn't all of it and, judging from the look on Adam's face, he wasn't deceived for a moment.

There were a lot of things she had liked that Zac had scorned, Micky recalled miserably. He had never understood her passion for gardening for one thing, and he had been totally unsympathetic when she had told him how much she was missing her parents. The memory left a sour taste in her mouth, dulling the bright blue of her eyes and drawing the fine skin tight over her high cheekbones, giving her face a hard, bitter look.

When Adam drew in his breath sharply as if about to speak the sound brought Micky's head up swiftly. Only too aware that he had noticed the way she had avoided answering his question, she expected some sarcastic comment on the lines that she was still running away. Surprisingly it never came. Adam's eyes were steady on her drawn face, their expression unreadable yet somehow not hostile. Did she imagine it or was there a new warmth—perhaps even sympathy in their hazel depths? For a second she felt she *could* tell him, but then Adam spoke and the moment had gone.

'One thing that's always intrigued me,' he said lightly, lowering himself into a chair and lazily stretching his long legs out in front of him. 'That bouquet I brought for your mother—wherever did you get the meaning of the flowers from?'

And before Micky quite realised the skill with which he had skated over the dangerous ice of the subject of Zac she found herself laughing and, sitting opposite him, began to explain how, frustrated in her serious interest in gardening, she had resorted to reading everything she could find on the subject in the local library and so had come across the old Victorian book on the language of flowers which had led her to interpret the message in the flowers Adam had brought.

From there it was an easy step to tell Adam about the start of it all, the blissfully happy holiday she had spent with an aunt and uncle, working in and learning all about the huge overgrown jungle of a garden at the back of the cottage they had just bought. She even admitted to her secret ambition to find such a wilderness of her own and make her perfect garden of it.

'We didn't have a garden before, you see, just a bit of a lawn, but I always had plants inside the house. Then when we moved——'

The sigh wouldn't be suppressed. Just for a moment she was that younger Micky seeing the huge garden for the first time, thinking that this at least was something good that had come out of all the change and upheaval, only to be told that her parents wouldn't hear of her doing the work herself—they could afford to pay someone to do it now.

Adam moved suddenly, getting out of his chair to change the record and, jolted out of her reverie, Micky altered her position too, sliding on to the rug before the fire, feeling the need of the warmth to ease the chill of sadness that had invaded her mind. For a long moment Adam studied her face, his eyes narrowed thoughtfully.

'Why don't you go home, Midge?' he asked quietly. 'You can make it work if you try.'

Micky shook her head vehemently. She couldn't, not yet. She wasn't ready—and she was scared. What if it didn't work out?

'Stop pushing me!' she cried to cover the fear. 'I told you I won't be bullied!'

'I am *not* bullying you!' Adam's voice had hardened ominously. 'I'm trying to get you to see sense.'

A cold pain stabbed Micky's heart at the destruction of the easy peace there had been between them. She had felt comfortable and relaxed but that feeling had been an illusion. Adam had just been biding his time, lulling her into a false sense of security before returning to the attack, she thought unhappily, and because there was still that sneaking suspicion at the back of her mind that he might have purely mercenary motives for what he was doing, seeing her purely as the heiress to Dennison's, she felt betrayed and deceived and rushed blindly on to the offensive.

'Just why are you so damned determined that I should do what *you* want? What business is it of yours if I see my parents or not? You said you'd play straight with me but I haven't seen any sign of it yet. I told you everything but you——'

'Micky!' Adam cut in sharply. 'I will explain if you'll just let me get a word in—just calm down, you impossible child!'

If there was one phrase guaranteed to take all the fight out of her it was that. *Child*, she repeated to herself, letting the pain wash through her. Impossible child. Such a short time before she had opened up to him and he had listened, giving his time and attention unstintingly so that she had felt he was really seeing her as a person—until he slapped her back into her place with that derisive phrase.

'I don't think I want to hear your explanations,' she muttered through a haze of hurt resentment.

'Why not?' Adam was dangerously angry now, the coldly controlled voice sending a shiver down Micky's spine. 'For God's sake, you're not still under the illusion that I want to marry you for your money, are you?'

It had had to come. There had to be a showdown some time. Adam had never mentioned the words she had flung at him on that first night but it was impossible that he should have forgotten them. If only it could have happened earlier, when she could have responded angrily and got away unscathed, untouched except by relief that her fears had been unfounded. But the wave of desolation that swept over her now told her it was already too late for that. Her shoulders slumped and her head drooped like that of a puppet with its strings cut, and she heard Adam's next words dimly through the grey fog in her head.

'I don't know who or what gave you that crazy idea in the first place, but I think it's time you forgot it once and for all. The reason for my involvement in all this is quite simple—your father asked for my help.'

Micky's head came up sharply at that, her eyes widening in shock and confusion.

'My father!' she gasped. 'I don't understand—why should Dad——?'

The words wouldn't form properly; her tongue felt strangely thick and clumsy. Adam came to sit on the chair near her, holding her transfixed with the intensity of his gaze.

'Because he was damnably worried about you,' he said coldly. 'He said you were impossible—headstrong, stubborn, aggressive—he couldn't get near you, and he thought I might be able to.'

'You?' It came out on a croak of disbelief and Adam laughed cynically at the sound.

'You might find it hard to believe, but your father thinks we're near enough the same generation. He thought you might talk to someone nearer your own age when you wouldn't talk to him.' Again came that wry ironical smile. 'It seems he was a trifle over-optimistic.'

'I've talked to you!' Micky protested defensively. 'He only asked you to *talk* to me—not to play God! If you hadn't interfered that night, Dad would——'

'He would have backed down,' Adam cut in icily. 'I know—I saw it in his face—but that wasn't what you needed. It was time that someone stood up to you, forced you to face the consequences of your own actions. You wanted everything your own way—just as you do now.'

'That's not true!'

'Isn't it? Damnation, Micky!' Adam exploded suddenly. 'You're so caught up in your stupid pride that you can't see what you're doing! You want your parents to come to you—you won't even meet them half-way.'

Headstrong, stubborn, aggressive, the description—her father's description!—reverberated painfully in Micky's thoughts. Adam must have had those words in mind when they met, which explained the strange intonation, the coldly assessing look on his face—and her dress and behaviour could only have reinforced his already low opinion of her! She wished she could die, or that the ground would open and swallow her up. She had never known her father felt like that. She'd been too blind to see how bad things had become.

Unable to meet Adam's eyes, Micky stared into the heart of the fire and her voice was very low when she finally spoke.

'It wouldn't work,' she said slowly. 'I can't go back—I don't fit in. It's not my world, Adam!'

'Did you ever give it a chance?' The question came with an intensity that rocked her back on her heels for a second. Adam shook his head almost sadly. 'I thought you had more guts than that, Micky. You gave in too easily. You *let* yourself feel different and out of place—you didn't *try*! You have to fight for what you want—you told me you were born fighting.'

'Dad said that.' Did Adam remember everything she'd ever said? He had an uncanny ability to recall her exact words and quote them back at her. Micky wished he hadn't been quite so quick to remember that particular phrase. Seen in the light of that other description, the one Adam had flung at her only minutes before, her father's teasing comment had a new and decidely uncomfortable sting in its tail.

'I don't really want to fight.' It was just a whisper, but Adam caught it and his expression altered subtly, losing some of the anger but none of the hard, determined purpose that darkened his eyes.

'But you fought me,' he persisted forcefully. 'You're still fighting.'

Micky's head swung round to face him at last.

'You're different!'

One corner of Adam's mouth quirked up into a strange half-smile.

'Coming from you, that sounds suspiciously like a compliment, Miss Dennison. Could I have it in writing?'

Why had she said that? *What* had she said? How was Adam so different? In a daze Micky heard him ask exactly that question. The hazel eyes were fixed on her face, very deep and dark in the light of the single lamp that lit the room, and inexplicably Micky was reminded of the moment she had opened her eyes after her accident and had looked up into Adam's face in just this way, seeing the strength and encouragement she needed there in his eyes, as she did now. In that moment she felt she could trust him with her life and knew that only the absolute truth would do.

'I don't think I was ever really fighting you. I think I was fighting myself.'

Which was as near as she could get to the truth, because in the moment she had looked into his eyes and felt that overwhelming trust she had also known that she *was* still fighting, but now she was fighting something very different from the admission of her own mistakes. It was something that went far deeper than anything she had ever known before; something that, if she let it, could take over her mind, her heart, her life. She was fighting the fact that slowly and insidiously Adam had become a vital part of her life in a way that defied description by any such inadequate term as friendship. It had started in those early days when she had come to expect, almost to welcome his silent presence in the car behind, and it had slowly been growing ever since until now she couldn't imagine how it had felt to exist without Adam in her life.

Micky started violently as a hand touched her hair very lightly.

'I thought you'd never say it,' Adam murmured softly and Micky's heart contracted at the warmth in his voice.

The long hand ruffled her hair gently, the gesture so openly friendly and affectionate after the distance there had been between them that Micky smiled her delight straight into Adam's eyes. Immediately he froze, his hand stiffening on her hair as he studied her face, searching deep into her eyes as if trying to reach behind them and draw her thoughts out to him.

'Don't slam the door on the new life, Micky,' he said soberly. 'Give it a chance—see what it has to offer. Let those barriers down and meet people half-way. You never know, you might be pleasantly surprised.'

'As I was with you.'

She hadn't even known she was going to say that, it had just slipped out, and to judge from Adam's expression he was as surprised by her words as Micky herself. But then a smile came swiftly, lighting his whole face with a genuine pleasure that was somehow every bit as disconcerting as her own admission.

'I think that's another compliment—I am doing well tonight! Whatever happened to the big bad wolf?'

The glance Micky slanted at him was deliberately mischievous.

'He huffed and he puffed and he blew my house down,' she said lightly, and saw Adam's smile widen to a grin of delighted amusement.

'So you see yourself as a little pig, do you? It figures; you've been screaming "I will not let you in" ever since I first met you.' Abruptly the grin faded, leaving Adam's face looking sombre and strangely empty without it. 'Why now, Micky?' he asked. 'Why the change? Did I really blow down your house of straw?'

House of straw—Micky's mood sobered as swiftly as Adam's had done at the words. Yes, that was all it had been. Her defiance, her anger, her hostility, they had all been just barriers built up around herself, as fragile and unfounded as the little pig's house, and she had retreated behind them, cutting herself off rather than admit that, deep down, she was afraid.

Adam was waiting for her answer to his question, waiting quietly and patiently, and yet there was an underlying tension about him, a tautness of face and body that communicated more clearly than words could ever do the fact that the answer she gave now was somehow more important than anything that had gone before, important in a way she couldn't quite grasp. And because she couldn't understand she was suddenly nervous, pushing the question away until she was ready to answer it.

'Why does it matter so much to you?' she asked slowly, and although it was a question she had asked so many times before, this time it was different. There was a new sharpness in her need to know the answer. The question had become more complex than simply discovering his reasons for being involved. Suddenly it mattered very much to know how he *felt*.

Adam lifted his shoulders in an offhand gesture that also managed to convey a hint of uncertainty.

'Funny you should ask,' he drawled laconically. 'I've been beginning to wonder myself. I started out simply trying to help a friend, a man I've come to admire and respect in the short time I've know him. He had this rebellious brat of a daughter who was making his life hell and——' Again came that thoughtful shrug, 'I had first-hand experience of the way families can break down.'

Memories clouded Adam's eyes, drawing all the life from them.

'I'd seen what that feud did to my father, how the regret, the guilt for what he'd done blighted what was left of his life and I didn't want that to happen to anyone else. Damnation, Michaela!' he declared harshly. 'I had to tell my father that Nina was dead!'

Shocked by the sudden roughness of his voice, Micky reached out a hand towards him in an instinctive gesture of sympathy then stopped suddenly, the movement uncompleted. Michaela, he had said, no longer Midge, not even Micky, and the use of her full name stung like the lash of a whip.

'You don't pull any punches, do you?' she breathed shakily.

'Not with you, anyway,' Adam admitted wryly. 'Which, believe it or not, isn't quite how I'd planned to handle things. I'd meant to be objective, uninvolved and so very reasonable, but when I met you all my good resolutions flew out of the window. I couldn't be objective about you no matter how hard I tried; you got under my skin from the start. You seemed such a cocky, defiant little creature, flinging your provocative remarks at me like a challenge, and I got angry. I wanted to take you down a peg or two—that's when I told your father to stand up to you and let you make your own mistakes—and, I hoped, learn from them. I felt sure your ultimatum over Zac was just another challenge. I never really believed you'd go, or if you did you'd soon come running home with your tail between your legs.'

As Micky stiffened at his words Adam slanted a rueful, self-derisory glance in her direction.

'I know. I miscalculated there. You've got more determination than I gave you credit for. When you didn't come back your parents were frantic with worry, so I made enquiries and found out where you were and came to see you—as I've said, I felt responsible for some of what happened. But you were still fighting and I have to admit that I was intrigued to find myself *enjoying* the way you stood up to me. You were a spitting, screaming little cat of a thing, but you had spirit and just once or twice you let that mask slip and showed that underneath that appalling make-up and the play-acting you were surprisingly vulnerable.'

Micky bit her lip hard. She should have known that those momentary weaknesses would not have evaded those keen, observant eyes. Unnerved by the way he had seen right through her, she over-reacted strongly.

'So you decided to break me down!' she declared aggressively and heard Adam sigh his exasperation.

'For God's sake, child, I don't want to *break* you! I've seen enough yes-men and flatterers to make me value someone with a mind of her own. I just wanted you to see that you were using that fighting spirit of yours destructively, hitting out at the people who cared for you and twisting yourself up in knots as a result. Once you'd let your guard down enough for me to see behind it, it was obvious that all the clever talk was just a front, and deep down inside you were eaten up with unhappiness. That's when I finally lost my grip on any impartiality I had left. Suddenly it became important to take away all that unhappiness. You were wasting your life fighting against things when you should have been fighting *for* what you wanted. Look at you——'

The sudden softening of Adam's tone caught Micky unawares so that she was unable to resist when his hand came under her chin, lifting her face towards his. One long finger flicked contemptuously against an elaborately painted eyelid.

'You're a very pretty girl, but you cover up that prettiness with all this muck, and your hair——'

A coolly disparaging look flickered over the offending locks, a frown darkening Adam's face as he considered the gaudy, over-bright shade.

'What colour is your hair naturally?' he demanded abruptly.

'Sort of brown.'

The answer came out stiffly and ungraciously, making Micky's heart sink at the sound, but her feelings were too confused for her to be able to impose any control over her voice. The touch of Adam's hand on her cheek was doing strange things to her pulse-rate and she was hopelessly unprepared for the sudden surge of pleasure the casually-spoken compliment brought her. The colour came and went in her cheeks as she struggled for composure.

'Why the hell do you dye it?'

There was no answer she could give him without her voice betraying her completely. She could almost hear Zac urging her not to be so stick-in-the-mud, to try something different—and like a fool she had done as he suggested. She had done so many stupid things for Zac, blinding herself to her real needs, her real self, trying to be the girl he wanted, and in doing so she had betrayed herself.

With half her mind Micky heard the song on the record Adam had chosen:

'Some people live with the fear of a touch
And the anger of having been a fool'

and the words came so close to the way she was feeling that she was seized with a sudden suspicion that he might have chosen just that song quite deliberately. Her eyes burned and she screwed them tightly shut against the tears.

'Midge?'

Adam's soft use of his personal, affectionate name for her proved Micky's undoing. With a small, choking cry she abandoned all hope of restraining her tears and simply let them flow, too weak, too desolate even to wipe them away. But because they were also tears of anger at herself, at her blindness, her stupidity, her hopeless self-deception, her hands clenched convulsively into fists, her bitten nails digging into her palms as she succumbed to the anguish inside herself.

There was a rustle of movement beside her as Adam slid to the floor at her side. Warm hands closed over her fists, easing the tightly curled fingers open and smoothing the bruised flesh with a gentleness that was reminiscent of that brief caress in the restaurant before strong arms came round her, gathering her close up against the firm, dependable wall of his chest in a way that was both comforting and supportive. In the instinctive movement of a small creature seeking the safety of its home Micky turned her face into his shoulder and wept out her shame and misery like a child.

Adam simply let her cry. Not a word was spoken until her sobs slowed, but all the time he held her firmly but gently, his arms and the warmth of his body enfolding her like a protective cocoon until she felt ready to face the world—and herself—again. At last, on a final gasping sigh, Micky's sobs ceased and she lay exhausted against Adam's shoulder, sniffing inelegantly, reluctant to move from the comfort of his arms.

This was how she had felt on the night of her fall, she thought hazily, safe and warm and peaceful, and this time there was no panic, no struggle for release when she discovered whose arms held her. She couldn't be more aware of the fact that she was in *Adam's* arms and it was that knowledge that added to rather than destroyed her sense of peace.

Turning her head slightly so that she could look up into Adam's quietly watchful eyes, Micky wished that she could find some way to tell him how much his silence had meant to her. She had been so weak, so completely defenceless that she would have done anything he asked if he had said a word. What better chance would he have had to push home his advantage, make her promise to go home—and he hadn't taken it. Her appreciation of his consideration went so deep that she was incapable of finding the words to express it and instead took refuge in more trivial matters.

'I've made your shirt all wet,' she murmured and felt as well as heard the laughter that shook his body.

'It'll dry,' he responded lightly, his breath warm on

her cheek. Then he chuckled again, a soft, friendly sound that lifted Micky's spirits just to hear it.

'You look like a baby panda,' he told her, grinning wickedly at Micky's consternation. 'Did you know you have two wonderful black eyes?'

Jerking upright, Micky stared at the tell-tale streaks of black mascara on Adam's formerly immaculate shirt and her hand went up to her face, coming away stained at the fingertips. With a cry of embarrassment she pulled herself from Adam's arms and fled towards the bathroom.

CHAPTER NINE

MICKY watched the swirl of water that carried the last of the elaborate make-up down the drain with a strong sense of satisfaction. She had finished with such overdone effects, she vowed, raising her head to meet the eyes of her own reflection in the mirror. Since she had started eating properly again the hollows in her cheeks had filled out, and without the mask of eye-shadow and mascara her eyes looked soft and vulnerable and very, very blue. But her over-enthusiastic scrubbing had left her skin pink and glowing, and the tip of her nose was unflatteringly shiny.

A very pretty girl, indeed! she thought satirically. She looked like a schoolgirl! Some women might envy her her youth, but right now Micky felt she would willingly trade several years of that youth for an ounce of sophistication or glamour, something that would make Adam see her as something other than the child he had so often compared her to.

But what else could she expect? After all, she had set out to prove herself to be nowhere near Adam's age. She had only herself to blame if events had rebounded on her.

Adam was standing by the window staring out at the lights of the city spread out below him, his hands pushed deep into his trouser pockets and his shoulders slightly hunched as if he was deep in thought. He swung round swiftly as Micky hesitated in the doorway, his eyes going straight to her pink-cheeked face and narrowing sharply in evident surprise. With an effort Micky squashed down a pang of disappointment. She was acutely conscious of the fact that this was the first time Adam had seen her without the heavy mask of make-up—and if the bemused expression that crossed his face was anything to go by he was not over-impressed by the sight!

'Here you are!' she declared with forced brightness. 'The plain, unvarnished truth at last—the real me!'

The abstracted smile that was Adam's response to her flippancy came and went swiftly like an automatic sign flicking on and off, and it touched only his mouth, never reaching his eyes. Micky's spirits plummeted even lower as on a second and more painful twist to her heart she admitted that, although she had no hope of stunning him with her beauty, just for a moment she had dreamed . . . Micky snapped off that foolish train of thought as, like a man emerging from a dream, Adam shook his head slightly and took a step towards her.

'I was wrong,' he said slowly and, hypersensitive to everything about him, Micky caught the faint unevenness in his voice. 'I said you were pretty but you're more than that . . .'

Suddenly it was as if everything was happening in slow motion. Dazedly Micky watched Adam come closer, reading his intention in his eyes, and she made no move to distract him or to break the mood because she knew with absolute certainty that what he wanted she wanted too.

As if in a dream she saw his arms reach out to her and without quite being aware that she had moved she found that she had stepped forward into them, confident and unafraid, without a thought of how or why or what might be, feeling only that this was right and good and somehow inevitable. Just the feel of those arms around her waist, their touch so very different from the gentle strength with which he had held her earlier, sent a sweet excitement flooding through her, warming her blood and setting every nerve-end alive.

When Adam's lips touched hers, Micky's response

was one of purely physical delight. She felt as if she was melting against him, her bones softening and her body limp with desire. Her heart soared with the knowledge that she was wanted, the presence of that hard, lean length against her a source of intense joy mixed with a burning frustration, because deep down inside her she knew that she wanted to be even closer still.

Adam muttered her name, his voice thick and rough, but Micky could only sigh a wordless response. Her lips parting, she returned Adam's kiss with a passion that equalled his, the warm excitement turning to a clamorous need that was so intense it was almost a shaft of pain. The pang of wanting was so new and unexpected that she cried aloud at the sharpness of it—and then almost choked on the sound, her mind reeling with shock.

This was desire, this wanting so much that it hurt—but she had known nothing like this before, felt nothing like this with Zac! Zac had never aroused this sweetly agonising need in her, and so—oh God, with Zac she had been living a lie!

Blindly Micky reached for Adam, wanting to obliterate the horror of her thoughts in the ecstasy of his embrace, but he had caught her momentary hesitation. Perhaps he read her thoughts in her eyes, perhaps in her anguish she had even spoken Zac's name out loud, she didn't know, but whatever the cause, his reaction was immediate and devastating. He released her at once, taking a swift step backwards, his expression suddenly withdrawn and remote. In desperation she stood on tiptoe to press her lips against his but his mouth closed against her, rigid and unyielding, bruising her—but the real pain was in her heart.

'I'm sorry.' It came out stiffly, with a polite formality that was bitterly ironic after the passion there had been between them only seconds before. 'I didn't mean that to happen,' Adam went on, then abruptly his unnatural composure broke completely. 'Damn you, Midge!' he exclaimed harshly. 'What is it about you that makes me behave like this? I've always thought of myself as a rational sort of man, but there's nothing rational in the things I've been doing lately. If any other woman had made it so blatantly obvious she couldn't stand the sight of me as you did at the beginning, I'd have said goodbye and good riddance and thought myself well free of her. But instead I find myself hounding you. Yes, I admit it, calling at your flat long after any sane man would have given up, following you night after night simply to make sure you were safe. God, I must be crazy!'

Well, that makes two of us, Micky answered him in the privacy of her own thoughts, because she was beginning to have definite doubts about her own sanity too. She couldn't seem to stay in the same mood for more than five minutes at a time and now, in spite of the shock of having discovered a distinctly unsavoury fact about herself, in spite of the pain of Adam's sudden withdrawal, all she could think was that he had called her a woman and had put an interpretation on those nightly vigils other than his openly declared desire to help her father. His anger—directed at himself, not really at her—revealed an involvement beyond the objective concern he claimed. She didn't question the happiness that knowledge brought but simply let it happen.

'I brought you here to talk to you,' Adam was saying. 'Instead——'

The hazel eyes swung back to Micky's face again. Although touched by doubt and confusion, they were clear, direct and honest, like the mind behind them—how could she have ever thought them cold? As if of its own volition, one hand reached out and Adam stroked the backs of his fingers softly down her cheek.

'How *could* you hide yourself behind all that rubbish?' he asked, all anger gone, leaving only a gentle incredulity. It was a rhetorical question, not really needing an answer, but she wanted to give him one.

'Because I was a fool,' she declared honestly, meeting his eyes without fear or hesitation. 'Because I felt inadequate and inferior and out of my depth. I didn't know how to handle the changes that had happened, and instead of facing up to them and learning how to cope I rejected everything, deliberately setting out to alienate myself from the people who might have helped me. But I was only covering up the fact that I was afraid. That's why the make-up, the clothes, the hair—everything. You've made me see that.'

For a long, long moment Adam said nothing, then he shook his head slowly. 'You've seen it for yourself,' he said softly.

'With your help,' Micky insisted. 'You saw through it all, didn't you—as you saw through Zac,' she added shakily, a memory waking in the depths of her mind. 'That night—you said something about his nasty little game. You knew.'

Micky couldn't go on. She knew she hadn't expressed herself at all clearly, but the look in Adam's eyes told her he had understood everything she had been trying to say in spite of the hesitations and confusion.

'I know his type.' The low voice was very gentle. 'And I knew he'd hurt you. The Zacs of this world take what they want from other people, then abandon the broken pieces when they move on to fresh excitement.'

Adam stopped abruptly, his expression growing hard and bleak for a moment, then he straightened his shoulders as if coming to a decision and held out his hand to her.

'Come and sit down, Midge. There's something I want to tell you.'

His arm slid around Micky's shoulders in a casual, friendly gesture as they moved towards the settee and he did not remove it when they were sitting side by side. Micky made no attempt to move away either. It seemed right to have his arm around her, the warmth and weight of it reviving the glowing sensation she had experienced earlier. She was almost overwhelmed by a longing to cuddle closer and rest her head against his shoulder, but the memory of his earlier withdrawal held her back and when he spoke his words drove all such thoughts from her mind.

'You've met Lauren,' he said and the cold, harsh note in his voice chilled Micky so that she tensed, her mind full of the scene in the restaurant.

Suddenly she was not at all sure she wanted to hear what Adam was going to say, not if it concerned a woman she had instinctively disliked on sight. She was startled to hear Adam's sudden chuckle, glancing at him in confusion to catch the smile that had wiped the closed, shuttered look from his face.

'Oh, Midge, you're so transparent!' Adam laughed. 'You didn't like her, did you? It's written all over your face—and you're right,' he added, his expression darkening again. 'Lauren is not the most lovable of women, thought I have to admit I once thought she was.'

The hand that lay on Micky's shoulder clenched suddenly.

'We were lovers for almost a year,' Adam declared harshly, but it was not the sudden savagery of his tone that shocked Micky but the agonising pain that tore at her in a burning fury of feeling, making the touch of jealousy she had experienced in the restaurant just a pinprick by comparison.

'When?' she managed through a throat that was suddenly dry and tight.

'Years ago. I was just twenty and she was five years older. She was a young man's fantasy, sophisticated, experienced, glamorous—and very, very sexy.'

'She still is.' It was just a whisper, but Adam heard and nodded grimly.

'And she still has the power to attract men to her like moths to a flame. She was always like that, always surrounded by admirers. She could have had any man she wanted, but she chose me. I couldn't believe it. I was crazy about her—I lived and breathed Lauren. I wanted to marry her; I even bought the ring—but by then Lauren didn't want to marry me—thank God!'

Micky flinched at the black cynicism in Adam's voice. She felt as if she were being twisted into knots inside; her own painful memories of Zac's careless dismissal of her protestations of love getting tangled up with her feelings about the things Adam was telling her, intensifying them, making her hurt for him.

'She didn't love you?'

'Love!' Adam's laugh was harsh, totally devoid of humour. 'I doubt if she knew what the word meant—even if she did, there was a much more important one in Lauren's vocabulary—money. She thought that in me she'd also got Rochford Electronics. She might even have married me if that had been the case, but she reckoned without my father. I didn't own any part of the company. I never did until this year. I was just employed there, starting at the bottom and working my way up, learning the business as I went. I was paid for the job I did—nothing more.'

He'd told her that before, Micky recalled, her conscience pricking her savagely. 'Whatever he gave us we had to earn,' he'd said, and, enmeshed in her own prejudice, she hadn't realised how important that was. Any last remaining shreds of her view of Adam as a man born to moneyed ease shrivelled and died. He had worked hard to get where he was and had proved himself worthy of the position he held. Everything she had ever heard about old John Rochford told her that he would never have put his son in charge of the American company if he hadn't had complete confidence in his ability to handle the job.

'When Lauren discovered that all I had to live on was a very basic salary, she broke off the relationship and turned her attention elsewhere. Within a month she was engaged to some other poor fool with more money than sense, and no awkward old father to stop her getting her hands on the cash. They were divorced three years ago. For a long time I saw nothing of Lauren but just lately—since I inherited the company—she's been taking rather more than a passing interest in me again.'

'Do you still feel anything for her?' Micky forced herself to ask, though if she was honest she had to admit that she really didn't want to know the answer.

'Good God, no! My infatuation died almost as soon as I was free of her. I may have been blind once, but when my eyes were opened I saw her for the hard, money-grabbing bitch she was and I was glad to be rid of her.'

Harsh and savagely spoken as Adam's words were, they set Micky's heart singing, soaring like a bird freed from its cage, because they swept away any last remaining doubts of her own. The disgust that thickened his voice when he spoke of Lauren, the obvious loathing he felt for the way she had wanted him only for his money, convinced her that he could never, even for a second, have considered Micky herself as simply a means to acquiring Dennison's. The rush of joy that followed that conclusion made her head swim.

'No regrets?' she asked, happiness lifting her voice so that Adam glanced at her sharply, but he answered her question quietly and with the direct honesty she had come to expect from him.

'I regret that I wasted so much time with her,' he said slowly. 'I regret that I ever made love to her. And I regret most of all the way I gave my love foolishly to someone who wasn't worthy of it.'

As she had done with Zac. Micky almost moaned aloud as her mind was flooded with memories. *Not now!* She didn't want to think of Zac now! But she couldn't drive the pictures from her mind though the mental echo of Zac's careless, 'We had some fun, Mick, but it was no big deal,' made her want to fold her arms round her body to hold herself together.

'Of course such things don't matter as much for a man as they do for a woman,' she blurted out, her pain loosening her guard on her tongue, and was quite unprepared for the gleam of cold anger that suddenly lit in Adam's eyes.

'You said something like that once before,' he said tightly. 'I didn't agree with you then and I still don't now.'

Micky almost felt she could believe him. She *should* have been able to, after all, his honesty was one of the things she had come to admire in him. But Adam was only speaking theoretically; she knew from direct and very painful experience that it was *very* different for a woman. If she had had any doubts on that score, Tony's behaviour had swiftly disillusioned her.

She had talked to Tony, danced with him, glad to see a familiar face—a friendly face, she'd thought. But when he walked her home he had made it blatantly obvious that he expected much more than a good night kiss in return for his company. He had been openly disbelieving of her refusal, had mocked her with the crude statement that no one missed a slice off a cut loaf, had become angry and finally almost violent. It was only when, to Micky's overwhelming relief, Susie had arrived home that he had given up and, flinging the final insult that she was only another man's leavings, second-rate, shop-soiled goods, in Micky's face, had stormed out of the room.

Adam might regret having loved Lauren, but he would never have to endure something like that. The double standard still existed; once a girl was no longer a virgin she was considered cheap, fair game for any amorous male. Tony had proved that; why should Adam be any different? If she told him the truth, told him that she had gone into Zac's bed as blindly and stupidly as she had done everything else, would he still say it didn't matter? Her stomach lurched queasily at the question. She felt she knew the answer.

Beside her, Adam was shaking his head and on his face was a wry smile at his own thoughts.

'You've done it to me again,' he said drily. 'I don't know how it happens, but somehow when I'm with you I just don't behave like myself. For one thing, I've never told any other woman about Lauren.'

'So why did you tell me?' Micky asked slowly and felt the arm around her shoulder tighten strongly.

'Oh, Midge, can't you see?' Adam said gently. 'I just wanted you to know that you haven't got the monopoly on making mistakes.'

The silent hall was chill in the early light of a dull, grey morning but Micky didn't feel the cold. An excited restlessness pricked in her veins and although it was scarcely past six o'clock she was wide awake. In fact she'd hardly slept at all that night, her mind suddenly clear and calm and completely decided, and she was going to act on that decision this very morning—but there was something she had to do first. Adam had a right to know. She desperately *wanted* him to know, and she couldn't wait any longer to tell him.

The phone seemed to ring for ever, but at last she heard the click she was waiting for and tensed, uncertainty warring with happiness inside her.

'Hello?' Micky's heart leapt at the sound of Adam's voice. It sounded thick and blurred with sleep but sharpened immediately when she gave her name. 'Midge? What is it? What's wrong?'

'Nothing's wrong, Adam,' Micky assured him hastily. 'I'm sorry if I woke you, but I wanted you to be the first to know. I've made up my mind. I——' Micky hesitated then brought the words out in a breathless rush. 'Adam, I'm going home—and this time I'm going to make it work.'

Home. In the silence that followed her outburst she

felt a flood of joy wash through her. Home. It had such a wonderful, welcoming sound.

'I'm glad,' Adam said at last, and Micky could hear the smile in his voice though she couldn't see his face. 'And you will make it work, I know you will.'

In the deserted hallway Micky's face lit up, and unconsciously she rested her cheek against the receiver as if it had been Adam himself. This was why she had had to ring him. This was how she had known it would be—no triumph, no comment that he knew she would see sense in the end—just a genuine pleasure in her decision and her happiness, and his last remark had revealed his confidence in the fact that she was adult enough to see it through, and that was the most important thing in the world.

Her silence seemed to disturb Adam. Once more that sharper note crept into his voice.

'Midge, are you okay? You're not scared, are you? Don't worry, you'll be fine—but if you want any help I can——'

'No,' Micky put in swiftly and firmly. 'Thanks, Adam, but no. This is something I have to do on my own.'

'Good girl.' The low voice was warm with approval. 'I knew you wouldn't need me in the end. I'll be thinking of you anyway.'

'Adam!' Micky cried swiftly as she sensed he was about to put the phone down. 'There's something else—I—I want to thank you for all you've done. You can't know how much it's meant to me . . .'

Her voice trailed off awkwardly. She had wanted to say so much more, but the impersonal mechanism of the telephone inhibited her, drying up the words in her throat. For a few seconds there was a strange silence at the other end of the phone, and when Adam spoke again he sounded distant and reserved.

'It was no trouble, Midge. I'm glad I was some help. Just promise me one thing. Don't ever lose that fighting spirit of yours. That little spitfire is the Midge I've come to know——'

'That infuriating pest that buzzes round you incessantly?' Micky interjected quickly—too quickly and too flippantly, but there was no way she could stop herself. There was a distinct pause, one that lasted just long enough for her to regret her impetuousness.

'Something like that,' Adam murmured drily. 'I'll let you go now, you must have a lot to do. Good luck, Midge—I'll see you around some time.'

With hands that were suddenly lifeless Micky let the receiver drop back on to its cradle and stood for a long moment staring at it blankly.

Oh, *why* had she done that? Why had she jumped in on Adam in that way? Because she was scared, she admitted to herself; scared that he might just have meant 'the Midge I've come to know' and had never intended to use the all-important words that usually completed the phrase. She had wanted him to say 'the Midge I've come to know *and love*' and had been afraid that he wouldn't, and knowing that she couldn't bear it if he didn't, she had jumped in with both feet, cutting him off so that now she would never know. In acknowledging how much it would have meant to her to hear those words and how it would have hurt if she hadn't, Micky knew she was also acknowledging what had happened to her. Without quite being sure how it had crept up on her, she knew quite simply that she had fallen in love with Adam.

Despondently Micky slumped back against the wall, folding her arms tightly around herself. 'I knew you wouldn't need me in the end,' Adam's words repeated over and over in her head like the sound of a farewell, making her moan aloud. She didn't need Adam any more, at least not in the way he meant. He had helped her grow up, put her back on the rails, and from now on she could cope—or could she? Because in another totally different sense of the word she needed Adam more than ever. He was the centre of her world, her reason for living, the sun that brightened every day simply because he was in it. Her childish infatuation for Zac was a million miles away from what she felt for Adam. He had made her grow up, all right; she was no longer a child but a woman—and that woman loved Adam with all her heart.

And with her body too, Micky added miserably, recalling the passion the single kiss they had shared had roused in her, a passion that had been noticeably missing with Zac.

'Oh, Adam,' Micky sighed on a note of longing.

Adam—the first man, but not for her. There was a bitter taste in her mouth and an empty ache where her heart should have been. Adam was the first man she had ever really loved, but sexually Zac had been the first. She had given him her innocence, wasted it on a passing infatuation that she could now see had never been love at all, and all she had left was second-best—and Adam was worth much, much more than that.

Drearily Micky dragged herself back upstairs, all her joy in the day of new beginnings drained out of her. First or last, it didn't matter anyway, because Adam would never know. His casual goodbye told her that she meant no more to him than someone he had tried to help through a difficult time. She was still Bill Dennison's young daughter whom Adam had hoped to reconcile with her father. He had succeeded, achieved his aim, and as far as Adam was concerned that was that. She had been a problem to solve, a challenge he had called her, and he had put all the time and energy that he put into his business dealings into sorting out that problem. Now he would put it all behind him with the satisfaction of a job well done. But Micky knew that, for her, the problems were only just beginning.

CHAPTER TEN

'I THINK the pearls with this dress, don't you? Or perhaps this.' Amanda Dennison took another necklace from her jewellery box and held it up against herself. 'Micky, what do you think?'

'The pearls look lovely,' Micky assured her, adding honestly, 'and so do you.'

Mrs Dennison's face lit up at once, her smile wiping away the worried frown, and Micky's heart twisted at the thought of how easy it was to make her mother happy—at least it was now that she saw that the excessive fussing and preoccupation with appearances was just Mrs Dennison's own way of expressing her insecurity in the role of the wife of the owner of Dennison's. Micky's conscience pricked her at the thought of just how many other times she had failed to see that.

'You're right, the pearls are perfect.' Micky's mother fastened on the necklace with a new confidence. 'Though of course I can't match up to you, love. That blue looks wonderful on you.'

'We'll knock 'em dead, the pair of us!' Micky laughed, pushing her own doubts and fears to the back of her mind for her mother's sake.

But once in the car, trying to balance the awkwardly shaped parcel on her knee, she could not hold back those doubts any longer and her stomach clenched nervously at the prospect of the evening ahead.

In many ways it had been a long two months since Micky had moved back into her parents' house, but in others it seemed no time at all. She had learned a lot, seeing things with new eyes, no longer blinded by her own foolish prejudices, but it hadn't always been easy.

After the first ecstatic welcome, the euphoria of her homecoming had subsided into a time of adjustment on both sides with all three of them treading carefully, tentatively establishing a new basis for their relationship. Only in the last ten days or so had she begun to feel that they were getting somewhere. It was as if they had cleared away the rubble of the past and laid the new foundations, and now they could begin to build. At last there was a future to work towards, and Micky felt more confident and at ease with herself and the world than she had done for years. In fact, life would have been quite perfect if it was not for one thing—Adam.

Micky stared out at the darkening streets, oblivious of her parents' cheerful chatter in the front of the car. The little she had seen of Adam had given her no chance to adjust and build up a new relationship with him too. He had rung her on the first night and several times since then, and had called at the house once or twice, but some problem with production had taken him to America and kept him there for over three weeks, so Micky had never got beyond the more formal meetings they had had with her father and mother present.

In some ways she had welcomed her parents' presence, finding the sight of Adam such a mixture of exquisite joy and bitter pain that it closed her throat, leaving her incapable of saying a word. She had spent almost all the time in his company in a tongue-tied silence, simply watching him, drinking in every small detail about him until she felt that her heart would burst with the love that was in it.

Adam himself had treated her with his usual easy friendliness, showing no sign of suspecting that anything had changed. But then there was no reason why he should—*he* wasn't the one who had fallen in love. To him, Micky was still just her father's daughter and the most that she could hope for was that he regarded her too as a friend. The bitter irony of that stabbed at her cruelly. It was a wonderful feeling to know that she had someone like Adam, a friend she could trust and in whom she could confide; someone to turn to when those old feelings of inadequacy and uncertainty surfaced as they did from time to time. If she had met him earlier, had had his help and support in those first difficult days of adjustment, then perhaps she would not have made such a mess of things. But deep in her heart a rebellious little voice cried that she wanted so much more than mere friendship, and because of that his casual affability was as hurtful as it was welcome.

Well before Micky was mentally ready, the car drew up outside Adam's flat. It was impossible not to compare this visit with the other occasions on which she had come here—and there could hardly be a greater contrast with her arrival tonight than the first time she had set foot in the place—or, rather, not *foot*, Micky thought with a pang of sorrow at the memory of the way she had been held in Adam's arms, her face against his chest. For a moment she was strongly tempted to turn and run, but her parents were waiting, so she fixed a bright, false smile on her face and followed them into the hall.

It would have to be Adam's birthday party that was the first real test of how well she had adjusted the second time around, Micky thought; that all-important fact giving an added sharpness to a situation that already had her very much on edge. Nervously she smoothed down the silky skirt of her sapphire-blue dress, remembering her stunned amazement when she had first seen herself in it and had been unable to recognise the Micky she knew in the slim, stylish figure reflected in the mirror before her.

Externally at least, the change was dramatic. The low, square-cut neckline of her dress, supported by shoestring straps, revealed the finely shaped bones of her neck and shoulders and the delicacy of her long, slender arms, and its bright, clear colour picked up and heightened the colour of her eyes that glowed with an excited anticipation strongly mixed with an apprehensiveness she couldn't quite disguise.

The ugly red rinse had faded from her hair and what little had been left had been skilfully trimmed away so that her soft brown locks now hung smooth and sleek around her head like a silky, gleaming cap. Subtle make-up highlighted her eyes and cheekbones, and her hands—Micky smiled to herself. She was proud of the effort she had put into caring for her hands, ruthlessly restraining the urge to bite her nails so that, although two months were not enough to work miracles, even her mother could not deny that their appearance was greatly improved.

But underneath the new clothes, the altered appearance, some of the old Micky still lingered, making her legs distinctly unsteady beneath her as she made her way into the now-familiar living-room. The room was full of people, or so it seemed to Micky as she stood hesitating in the doorway. But then her eyes fell on the man she so wanted to see, and in that instant it was as if all the other guests had ceased to exist and there was just herself and Adam in the room.

He was standing in the middle of a small group of people, one arm slung casually around the shoulders of the girl next to him, his face alight with laughter at something one of his friends had just said. Seeing him like that, relaxed and at ease in his own world, the world of which she was such a new and uncertain member, Micky felt her breath catch in her throat at the impact of the lithe masculinity of his tall, powerful body. Subconsciously she had thought he would be more formally dressed, expecting to see the elegantly suited man she had first met, but his casual clothes, the brilliantly white shirt and black trousers a perfect foil for the rich colour of his hair, were those of his other personality, the Adam who made her forget that there was almost twelve years difference in their ages. She wished he had appeared in the other, more formal, persona tonight; perhaps then she might have been able to distance him slightly from her thoughts, achieve a control that would help her through the night. *This* Adam came too close to her heart. Micky sighed—so near, and yet so far, far away.

At that moment, Adam turned his head and saw them. Detaching himself from his friends, he made his way across the crowded room towards them, his smile taking in all three Dennisons, but privately Micky allowed herself the luxury of believing that one small part of it was meant for her alone. It was foolish, she knew. Indulging herself in this way was really only storing up more hurt for later. But she couldn't stop herself; she needed *something* to ease the aching emptiness that only Adam could fill.

Her 'Happy Birthday' sounding embarrassingly high and squeaky in her own ears, Micky managed a bright smile as she handed Adam the bulky, brightly wrapped present. She had agonised over her choice of gift, wanting to give him something special but not knowing what. It was only when she had remembered how, on her first visit to the flat, she had felt that it needed a plant or two to make it perfect that she knew she had hit on the right idea.

Her confidence in her choice vanished, leaving her feeling awkward and uncertain, when she saw Adam's stunned amazement at the sight of the dark fronds of greenery, but revived on a glow of happiness as his astonishment was swept away by a grin of pure delight.

'I might have known you'd come up with something different!'

The plant was taken from her and placed on a table, and the next moment she was gathered up in a powerful hug that lifted her off her feet and drove all the breath from her body. Then, before she had time to recover her mental equilibrium, warm lips were pressed against her cheek and a laughing voice whispered in her ear, 'And what's the message this time?'

In spite of her thudding heart and the struggle she was having to resist an impulse to fling her arms around his neck and hold him close, Micky managed a teasing smile. She had known he would remember, known he would ask, and had chosen the plant for just that reason. Her sparkling blue eyes looked up into the hazel ones that had haunted her dreams for weeks, her heart warming as she saw the gleam of amusement in them.

'It's a palm, which means victory,' she told him lightly. 'It was the nearest I could get to "you've won".'

And he would never know how hard it had been to resist any other message. It had seemed as if the shop had contained nothing but roses with their message of love, or carnations that spoke of an aching heart, and she had even picked up an ivy that promised eternal fidelity before the realisation that Adam would almost certainly ask its meaning had made her replace it hurriedly on the shelf.

Adam's expression had sobered abruptly, his eyes touched very faintly with doubt and uncertainty.

'*Did* I win, Midge?' he asked softly, his words meant for her ears alone. 'I've wondered sometimes if I did the right thing.'

And because she wanted to wipe that frown from his face, because she wanted him to believe she was idyllically happy, and most of all because he *had* done the right thing, Micky flashed him the most brilliant smile she could summon up.

'You did just the right thing,' she assured him.

The first half of the evening passed in a confused blur. Micky was swept away on a tide of introductions, conversation and laughter, constantly meeting new people, asking and answering questions until her mind was a whirl of images. She was surprised by the interest people took in her, delighted by the way they welcomed her into the circle of Adam's friends without a hint of condescension or hostility, and genuinely stunned by the number of compliments on her appearance she received from both men and women.

When she had a second to think, it was to reflect on just what she had been missing in those wasted years when she had refused even to try to get to know anyone in their new social circle, cutting herself off behind her self-created barriers. She was well aware of the fact that there were several people at the party that she had met at her parents' home, but to her newly-opened eyes they seemed like completely different people—or, rather, she admitted to herself, *she* was the one who had changed.

The new-found feeling of belonging was as intoxicating as the wine Micky drank, freeing her tongue and filling her with a liberating sense of well-being that was heightened and intensified by the happiness of knowing that Adam was there, supporting her, encouraging her, willing her to succeed. She knew that was how he felt without a word having to be spoken. He was constantly there at her side to introduce her to new people, staying just long enough to make sure she was holding her own before drifting away to perform his duties as host in some other part of the room. The fact that he did leave her told her more clearly than any words ever could that he had absolute confidence in her ability to cope.

Even when Adam wasn't near her she could feel his interest and concern, drawing the strength she needed from it. Once or twice she glanced up to find those light-coloured eyes fixed on her with a thoughtful, considering gaze, one that made her heart jolt uncomfortably. He looked as if he were staring at a complete stranger, someone he had never seen in his life before.

But then Adam became aware that she was watching him and his expression switched swiftly to one of warm approval. The smile he directed at her across the room was so private, so intimate, that her heart seemed to turn over as she smiled back at him, their eyes locking together in a suspended moment of perfect unity that excluded the rest of the world. In that moment Micky wondered how she had ever managed to exist without knowing Adam and loving him.

The elation of that moment, combined with the excitement of finding—and keeping—her feet in a world that had previously overwhelmed and frightened her, sustained Micky for some time. But after more than two hours the strain of the new experience began to tell. She felt her energy flag, and desperately needed a little time on her own to recharge her batteries in peace and quiet. As if summoned up by her thoughts, Adam appeared once more at her side, sliding an arm around her waist and drawing her away from the crowd.

'I need Micky's help,' he told the man she had been chatting to when he protested lightly that Adam was stealing the most fascinating girl in the room. 'She's lumbered me with this monstrous great Triffid of a plant, and I haven't the vaguest idea how to look after it, so I think it's time we had a private horticultural discussion.'

The corner that he had led her to was deserted and peaceful, and Micky leaned back against the wall with a sigh of relief.

'I've never talked so much in my life! My tongue must have holes worn in it. How did you know I needed to escape for a bit?'

'Telepathy,' Adam laughed. 'Either that or the fact that you've had a "Get me out of here" look on your face for the last few minutes. And of course I wanted to talk to you.'

'Oh yes, about the plant,' Micky put in hastily. She was glowing with happiness at the way he had inadvertently revealed that he'd still been watching her even though she clearly hadn't needed his help for some time, and that made her supremely conscious of the sight, sound and feel of him next to her as he lounged against the wall, his arm brushing hers.

'Forget the plant,' Adam growled unexpectedly. 'It was only an excuse, and you damn well know it. I wanted to get you to myself for a bit. You've hardly spoken three words to me all evening.'

With a sense of shock Micky registered a new and previously unheard intonation to Adam's voice. He sounded almost jealous! But he couldn't be! Switching to trivia to hide her uncertainty, she blundered on shakily.

'Have you thought where you're going to put it—the plant, I mean? I think it would look just perfect against the window.' Resolutely ignoring Adam's impatient sigh, she persisted, 'Or perhaps you could——'

'I don't give a damn about the plant!' Adam exploded in a savage undertone. 'For one thing it's rather foolish to decide where it will go in the flat when I won't be here for more than a couple of months.'

'You're moving?' It came out on a gasp.

Adam nodded. 'Out of town,' he told her curtly. 'I've been looking for a house for a while, now I think I've found one.'

Micky's heart sank to somewhere below the soles of her delicate leather sandals. If he was moving out of town she would see even less of him than she did now—and that was little enough. The few hours she had spent in his company had been as ineffectual in satisfying her need for him as a crumb of bread offered to someone who was starving.

'How nice,' she murmured inanely, trying desperately to keep up a pretence of polite interest. 'What's the house like?'

'For God's sake, Midge!' The muffled exclamation with its undertone of something verging on anger—or despair?—was the last thing Micky had expected. She didn't know what she had said to provoke it. Nothing in their rather stilted conversation could have caused the look of strain that seemed to stretch Adam's skin tight across his cheekbones. Micky fought an irrational flash of panic. She didn't know this Adam! The intense, forbidding stranger who towered over her, all the charm and the easy amiability stripped away, the changeable eyes darkened by some unreadable emotion, was suddenly totally alien to her.

'Midge,' Adam began again with an evident effort to control his voice, but whatever he had been about to say was interrupted by a group of his friends who approached them cheerfully, led by the girl Micky had seen with Adam when she first arrived—Miranda, Micky recalled. She had been introduced to her earlier and had amazed herself by being able to chat quite naturally, and even to find herself liking this woman whose name had been linked with Adam's.

For a split second Adam hesitated, his body stiffening as if he would have resisted when Miranda tried to draw him away into the middle of the room, and his eyes went to Micky's face in a look that awoke echoes of some elusive memory that she couldn't quite place. Then the moment was shattered as, with much laughter and teasing, he was pulled away to where a huge birthday cake illuminated by thirty brightly burning candles stood on a table.

From her corner Micky watched as Adam submitted to the urging of his friends and bent to blow out the candles, but it was as if a sheet of glass had come down between herself and the other people in the room. She could see them, hear their voices, but the sounds were blurred and she felt completely cut off from reality. She saw Miranda claim a birthday kiss, saw Adam respond to her fervent embrace without any sign of reluctance, and took advantage of the moment when his face was concealed by the other girl's to slip quietly from the room to be alone with her thoughts.

Adam's bedroom was pleasantly silent and cool after the smoky warmth of the party. Micky sank on to the bed and kicked off her shoes with a sigh. She felt drained and exhausted, every trace of the exhilaration that had filled her earlier seeping away until she was as limp as a rag doll without any stuffing.

Her mind wandered back over the night she had slept in this bed and the muddled feelings that had filled her when she thought of Adam. Her thoughts weren't much clearer now, she reflected ruefully. She was every bit as confused as she had been then—not about her own feelings, the intense joy of those tiny moments of sharing had left her in no doubt that her love was real and strong and as essential to her as the air she breathed. No, it was Adam who bewildered her; the Adam of a few minutes before, a man whose swift change of mood she couldn't interpret any more than she could the look he had given her before Miranda had dragged him away.

Away from the noise and crush of the party, Micky found she could remember why that look had seemed familiar. It had been on Adam's face when she had told him she didn't want to fight him any more, and again just before he had kissed her. It was impossible to define what it meant; to try to do so would be like trying to put a moonbeam under a microscope. In the space of a heartbeat she had seen confusion, uncertainty, hope, vulnerability, need and longing, and underneath it all some hidden flame that seemed like a tiny fragile spark of the fire that burned in her heart. But *she* knew that that fire was a hotly burning love—in Adam . . .?

'So this is where you've hidden yourself.'

Micky's head snapped up in shock. Absorbed in her thoughts, she hadn't heard the door open or Adam come into the room, soft-footed and silent as a cat. Hastily she scrambled to her feet, stammering out a stumbling explanation.

'I—I had a bit of a headache, so I needed to be quiet for a bit. I'm okay now. I'll——'

She broke off as Adam shook his head silently. He kicked the door shut behind him, leaning his broad shoulders against it, effectively cutting off her exit.

'Don't go,' he said softly, his eyes, dark and broodingly absorbed, fixed on her flushed face as if he wanted to etch the image of it on his memory.

'Adam,' Micky choked, disturbed and frightened by his strange mood. She couldn't read any of his thoughts in his face; couldn't drag her own eyes away from the hypnotic force of his.

'Don't be afraid, Midge,' the low, softly accented voice soothed her. 'I won't hurt you—I just want to look at you.'

This can't be happening! Micky thought dazedly as she stood transfixed by the searching gaze that moved down from her face and slowly, lingeringly, over her body. It isn't real, it can't be! Any minute now I'll wake up, and find I'm in bed and it's only this morning and the party hasn't happened yet and it's all been just a dream—or a nightmare—but for the life of her she couldn't decide which.

The sense of unreality had her so much in its grip that when Adam huskily told her to turn round she did so unthinkingly, turning slowly like a model, her movement unconsciously sensual, swirling her silken skirt around her slender hips and legs. It was as she came full circle to face him again that Adam sighed, his eyes going back to her face as if drawn by a magnet and incapable of looking anywhere else.

'I like your hair much better "sort of brown",' he said unevenly.

It was yet further evidence of the way he listened to—and remembered—the most trivial things she said, and it revived memories of the times of sharing, the frank openness there had been between them, an openness that they seemed to have lost, so that tears stung Micky's eyes, blinding her temporarily.

Adam's eyes narrowed swiftly as he caught the unnatural brightness in Micky's, and through a blur of tears she saw him hold out his hand in a gesture that was a curious mixture of imperiousness and diffidence, silently ordering—or asking—her to come to him.

In a dream she moved slowly across the thick carpet, and as soon as she was within reach his arms came round her, drawing her against him gently but irresistibly until she was cradled against his length, her body curved along the line of his chest and hip and thigh, the warmth of him burning into her through the silky material of her dress. It felt right to be there, right and natural and wonderful, and those feelings drove away the uncertainty and confusion that had filled her mind. She no longer worried what Adam felt or thought, no longer cared, and even as he bent his head she had lifted hers, so that their lips met with a sweet inevitability that made Micky feel she might faint with the sheer joy of it.

Her feet no longer seemed to be resting on solid ground; she might have been floating inches above the floor for all she knew. It *was* a dream, she told herself hazily. It was too good, too perfect to be true. No one got their heart's desire so easily. But no dream felt as firm and solid as the strength of Adam's shoulder's under her questing fingers, no fantasy was so tangible and warm, and the pressure of Adam's lips on hers was hard and forceful, no fleeting illusion.

With a sigh Micky abandoned herself to Adam's embrace. Illusion or not, it was what she wanted, what she needed, and she was going to savour it to the full. As she pressed closer Adam's hands slid down to her hips, pulling her hard up against him until she felt that their bodies must be permanently bonded together. When he kissed her again it was with a fierce, unrestrained passion that had her hands moving over his chest and shoulders in hurried, feverish caresses, wanting to touch every part of him at once.

When Adam moved to the bed, drawing her down with him, Micky made no protest. She was beyond any such thought, all her senses quiveringly alert to the taste of his mouth, the scent of his skin, the thick softness of his hair beneath her fingertips. He hadn't spoken a word, but somehow that intensified the other pleasures; Adam was so rarely at a loss for something to say that his silence now spoke volumes for the way he was feeling.

No longer content simply to be kissed, Micky pressed her own mouth on Adam's, responding blindly to the needs of her heart, clinging to him with an unrestrained ardour that brought a groan of pleasure from deep in his throat. She hardly recognised herself in the passionate, uninhibited woman who lay in Adam's arms. With Zac she had never been like this. With him, her responses had been clumsy and awkward and as Zac's impatience grew, so did her nervousness, until, on that final, appalling night, she had frozen completely. Her body had grown rigid and unyielding until he had flung her from him, his face distorted with dark anger, and declared that he was wasting his time with a girl who had nothing to give.

But now, held close in the cavern of Adam's arms, no such inhibitions spoiled the ecstasy of the moment. Her lips seemed to know instinctively how to kiss, her hands just where to touch to give most pleasure, and the clamorous need that Adam's caresses awoke in her was not the response of a cold or even a restrained woman. It built up from a nagging ache to a searing climax, mounting in intensity with every touch of his hands and lips until her whole body was consumed by an inferno of desire.

The straps of her dress had long since vanished from Micky's shoulders, the bodice sliding down to reveal her small, pale breasts, and there was no way she could suppress a moan of delight as Adam's fingers stroked over the soft, glowing flesh. The noise of the party in the other room had faded to a blur, both of them totally oblivious to the presence of the other guests or the passage of time, until the sound of a door opening and a voice calling Adam's name jarred them back to reality.

As Micky froze in shock Adam jack-knifed off the bed with a violent curse, his hands going automatically to smooth his dishevelled hair and fasten his gaping shirt as he moved hurriedly to the door. Micky never heard what explanation he gave to the person who had come looking for him; her mind was beyond focusing on anything beyond the pain and devastation she felt at the savagely abrupt ending to her happiness, her body racked by an agony of frustration.

Shakily she swung her legs over the side of the bed but made no attempt to stand up, knowing she would collapse if she did so. Her mind working on automatic pilot, she pulled her dress back up over her exposed breasts and brushed ineffectually at her hair just in case someone should come in. Then, lacking the strength of mind or body to do anything more, she sat on the edge of the bed, her eyes fixed on a patch of carpet just beyond her feet, and waited for Adam to return.

Her numbed brain didn't register the moment when Adam came back into the room, so the first knowledge she had of his presence was when he knelt at her side, taking her trembling hands in both of his and looking deep into her troubled blue eyes.

'Midge,' he whispered softly. 'Oh, Midge, what can I say that will make it right? I know I should say I'm sorry—but I can't. It wouldn't be true. I'm *not* sorry. I could never regret something so good.' One hand slid up to cup her cheek with infinite gentleness and his eyes were dark, warm pools in his face. 'You're so beautiful, little one, and you came to me so sweetly and . . .'

The words died on his lips as he saw the unnatural brightness of her eyes, the pallor of her cheeks. Beautiful! Micky's numbed brain was repeating. He had called her beautiful!

'Midge, don't!' Adam begged huskily, misinterpreting her reaction. 'Don't look at me like that. I can't regret it, but I *am* sorry if I hurt or frightened you. I wouldn't have done that for the world. I—oh God, Midge, you're so young—too young!'

'No!' It was a cry of pain and it stopped him dead, his head going back in shock. The hand he had snatched away from her face to clench in a gesture of impotent anger against fate uncurled, and reached out towards her again very slowly.

'You're not angry?' he asked in a voice that was hesitant with disbelief, and instinct told Micky how to respond.

'No,' she told him gently, turning her head so that she could press a kiss against his palm. 'I'm not angry or frightened, and I don't want you to say you're sorry because I'm not. But I would like you to explain. You've given me no warning, never even hinted that you——'

'How could I give you warning of something I didn't know myself?' Adam put in quietly. He moved to sit on the bed beside her, his arm around her waist, warm and strong. 'I told you once I wasn't quite rational where you're concerned, but I didn't realise just how irrational I'd become. I think it all started that time in the café when you tried so hard to pretend you didn't give a damn, and all the time you were bleeding to death inside.'

'And you saw through the act.' Micky's voice was very low. Adam's eyes lit with a tender warmth.

'You're not a very good actress, Midge. That was when everything got turned on its head and making you happy became as important as anything I wanted to do for your father. As I got to know you it became more important still—until nothing mattered but your happiness, because by then I'd become very fond of my little spitting wildcat.'

'You didn't show it!' Micky protested with a watery smile.

'You didn't exactly give me the chance,' Adam countered laughingly. 'I'd only got to look at you the wrong way and you exploded. But I cared what happened to you so I persevered. Then one night you took off that appalling make-up.' Adam's smile at the memory was slow and gentle. 'I couldn't believe my eyes. Suddenly the wildcat had disappeared and in her place was a very lovely young girl, one I couldn't keep my hands off. But when you panicked I knew I'd moved too fast, making no allowance for how young you were—so I backed off.'

He fell silent for a moment, giving Micky unwanted time to think. Adam had interpreted her reaction as one of panic, seeing it as evidence of her youth and inexperience—her innocence—and the thought stabbed at her savagely.

'Believe me, kitten, I had meant to wait, let things develop gradually,' Adam went on before she had time to regain some mental balance, 'but you were always in my mind. All that time in America I was thinking of you, wondering how you were coping, and tonight when I saw you so completely transformed, looking so beautiful—half the men here couldn't take their eyes off you! Well, I couldn't handle it. I was jealous, I didn't want to share you, and when I found you here alone I went a little crazy—but that's not the way I wanted it. I don't want to rush you into anything you're not ready for. I'm impatient because I'm so much older—but I can wait if you're what I'm waiting for. Midge, look at me.'

Obediently Micky turned her head and found herself looking into eyes so deep and dark that she felt she might drown in them.

'What I'm trying to say is that I want to see you, be with you, talk to you and find out if what I'm feeling can turn into something very special—but I need to know how you feel. So tell me, Midge, will you give it a try?'

The answer was there in the light in Micky's eyes before she could even form the words, because there was only one reply she could give. She had been offered a chance of a happiness she had only dreamed of before now and she was going to take it with both hands. If it was craven and not completely honest to push her private fears to the back of her mind and pretend they didn't exist then she was going to have to admit to being such a coward. Because there was no way she was going to risk the devastation of her hopes and dreams that she was sure would result if she told Adam the truth.

CHAPTER ELEVEN

'BUT where are we going?' Micky demanded, her eyes bright with excitement and impatience. The mysterious smile that was Adam's only response to her question intrigued and infuriated her. 'Tell me!' she insisted, and saw his grin widen.

'Wait and see,' he instructed calmly, then sighed in mock exasperation. 'Women! They're incapable of waiting for anything.'

'Won't you give me just a hint—*please*,' Micky begged, leaning forward to put her hand on Adam's knee and turning her most beguiling smile on him.

'No,' was the unmoved response, the adamant tone tempered with a smile. 'And don't try your seductive wiles on me, young lady. You'll find out when we get there and not before, so just sit back and enjoy the scenery.'

Frustrated, Micky glared at Adam in reproach but she sat back as he instructed and turned her attention to the countryside through which they were travelling. For the first week in October it was amazingly mild. The sun shone in a cloudless sky and the rich colours of autumn made the landscape a patchwork of green and gold. Perhaps autumn wasn't her least favourite season after all, Micky thought. She was loving every minute of this one anyway.

Suddenly Micky laughed out loud from the sheer joy of living. Every day seemed filled with a rare sort of happiness, so luminously clear and sharp that it was almost painful. The girl of last October had gone for good and the future stretched ahead of her, warm and welcoming and infinitely exciting. Only that morning she had studied herself in the mirror, taking stock. The mirror told her she had changed, but it was a transformation that went far deeper than the surface changes of sleek shining hair, feminine clothes and carefully tended nails. She was whole again, whole and strong and happy, living life to the full, sure of herself and at ease with the person she had become.

Micky's eyes slid to the man at her side, lingering on the strong lines of his profile etched against the car window. They had shared so much since the night of Adam's party, glorious, heady days filled with laughter and joy and for Micky each day was a new beginning simply because Adam was in it. There had been quieter times too, hours spent listening to music or just sitting, content in each other's company, and endless hours of talk, the exciting journey of discovery through each other's mind, drawing them closer every day until they had reached the point where it was almost unnecessary to talk, each of them anticipating the other's thoughts, with the uncanny skill of a mind-reader.

Her relationship with her parents had flowered too, though inevitably there had been setbacks and difficulties. It had not all been plain sailing. For one thing, Micky was beginning to feel restless. She needed to do something constructive with her time but she didn't know what, and her father still couldn't see that there was any need for her to work when he was quite happy to support her as he had always done.

When problems had arisen Adam had been there, but he never pushed her towards any particular decision, that was not his way, He listened, offered his own ideas, and then stood well back, letting her make up her own mind even if her decision went against what he had suggested, and in doing so he gave her the most precious gift of all—the freedom to be herself.

The car swung off the main road and headed up a smaller, narrow lane.

'Not long now,' Adam murmured and Micky sat

forward in her seat, burning with anticipation and curiosity.

When Adam had told her that he was taking the day off for her nineteenth birthday so that he could take her out, she had been delighted at the prospect of a full day in his company and had been dressed and ready well before the time he had given for their departure. It had already been an exciting morning with many wonderful presents to examine, notably the shining new car that her parents had given her, but it was Adam's gift that Micky looked forward to with the greatest anticipation. He had promised her something special and, knowing Adam, Micky had no doubt that it would be just that. So it had been something of a shock when he had arrived at the house empty-handed.

His face lighting with laughter at the disappointment she was not quite able to hide, Adam had told her that he *did* have a present but it wasn't one he could wrap up or even carry. He had ushered her out to the car with a promise to take her to see his gift, and a warning that she would have to be patient because they had a journey to make first.

She was trying to be patient—but the journey seemed to be going on for ever and she was in a fever if anticipation, longing to know what the 'something special' could be. There had been other small presents over the weeks, thoughtful, carefully chosen gifts—but never, Micky recalled with a pang of regret, never once had Adam given her flowers. Which was strange, because in every other respect Adam had been the perfect suitor. Generous, attentive, considerate, he had set out to court her from the start.

A slow, private smile spread over Micky's face. Old-fashioned it might be, but there was no other word to describe Adam's behaviour, and there was another, equally unfashionable word that fitted how she felt. Adam made her feel wanted, cared for, special. He made her feel cherished and, although he had never used the word, that came very close to being loved.

Adam's hand moved to change gear and his fingers brushed against Micky's leg as he did so, sending a tingle of excitement through her body.

This was how she felt every time he touched her, and Adam himself had never tried to hide the fact that his desire for her was every bit as strong as Micky's for him. When they kissed an incandescent flame lit up between them, sweeping aside all thoughts of moderation or restraint, on Micky's part at least. But on the occasions when the white-hot tide of feeling threatened to swamp them it was always Adam who drew back and defused the situation with a calming word.

At those times, with her body aching for him, Micky had wanted to cry out in protest, beg him not to stop, but her secret thoughts froze the words on her lips so that they died unspoken. She was well aware that Adam's careful restraint came from a concern for the innocent young girl he believed her to be, and that thought was infinitely disquieting. Adam had seen her walk out of her parents' house *with Zac*, and so Micky found it hard to believe that, unlike Tony and the others who had assumed that she and Zac were lovers long before it was actually true, he still thought her sexually innocent. It was the one grey area in a relationship otherwise based on total honesty and trust and she had determined again and again to tell Adam the truth, but each time her nerve had failed her.

'There!' Adam announced, bringing the car to a smooth halt. 'What do you think?'

Jolted out of her reverie, Micky glanced around her in some confusion. The car was parked beside a white-painted gate beyond which lay a path that led to the front door of a very beautiful house. Tudor in design, it had evidently once been a farmhouse and had clearly been recently and lovingly restored. Almost all of the wall around the door was covered in a climbing ivy, but beyond it the pale stonework glowed golden in the mellow autumn sun.

'Adam, it's lovely! But——' Adam's grin betrayed him, making her round on him sharply. 'It's yours, isn't it? This is the house you've bought.'

Adam nodded a trifle smugly. 'I didn't want you to see it until it was really ready. It was almost derelict when I bought it but it's just about habitable now. Want to see inside?'

'Please.' It was something of a struggle to maintain the note of enthusiasm in her voice. Micky was torn between a genuine longing to see the interior of the house and her unhappiness at the thought that very soon the frequency of Adam's visits would be severely curtailed. Since he had told her he was buying a house, Adam had rarely mentioned the subject again; in fact she had almost forgotten that he planned to move at all. Now she was brought up hard against the reality of that fact.

Together they wandered through the downstairs rooms, some of which were still untouched, empty shells with bare plaster walls waiting for the personal touches that would make them part of a home. But the rooms that were already furnished made her cry aloud in delight at the cool, understated effect of pale walls and soft muted colours in the carpets and curtains that contrasted with the rich warmth of wood in the furniture and, above her head, the dark beams on the ceiling. This was a place she could be happy in, she told herself. It had a welcoming, friendly feeling, just like the one she had always sensed in Adam's flat.

'It's beautiful,' she told Adam sincerely. 'Really, really lovely. I bet you can't wait to move in.'

And when he did, when she didn't see him as often as she wanted, well, then she could enjoy thinking of him in this wonderful house.

'I plan to be out of the flat by the end of the month—if I get one little problem sorted out first. Which leads me very nicely to your present.'

Micky was mystified. She had forgotten all about her birthday present in her enchantment with the house.

'I don't see what my present has to do with your move,' she said in confusion.

Adam's answer was to hold his hand out to her.

'Come with me,' he said softly, and with her hand in his he led her through to a large airy room at the back of the house from which french windows opened on to a large conservatory. Adam led her through the conservatory and paused to fling open a door at the far end.

'Happy birthday, Midge!'

Micky just stared. The warmth of the sun, the gentle chirp of sparrows on the conservatory roof, even Adam's still presence at her side all faded into a shimmering mist in a moment of pure magic. There was no beauty in the tangle of weeds and grass and overgrown shrubs that lay before her but to Micky it was the most wonderful sight in the world. Remembering that secret ambition confided to him so long ago, Adam had given her her own garden!

She turned to the man at her side, her hands reaching out for him wordlessly. But words weren't needed. Everything she felt shone in her eyes, and Adam gathered her close to him on a sigh of pure contentment.

'Just let it make you happy,' he whispered.

'Oh, it will!' Micky assured him. It already had. There could be no greater happiness than to know that he cared enough to choose something so perfect. Her joy was heightened by the knowledge that each day she spent working in the garden would be time spent close to Adam. No longer would the time she spent without him seem so unproductive. Adam's gift would make her feel useful and fulfilled.

'You can use the conservatory too,' Adam offered, adding casually, 'I did wonder if you'd like to make it more than a hobby. You could make yourself a florist with a difference. With your interest in the meaning of flowers you could offer a special service—messages in flowers, making up bouquets to say just what the customer wants.'

Micky had thought that there wasn't room in her heart for any more happiness, that it was already filled to overflowing; but the depth of Adam's understanding, his words catching up her own secret thoughts, took her breath away.

'Would you let me do that? After all it is your garden—your home.'

'*Your* garden,' Adam corrected firmly. 'And as to the other—well——' He reached out for her again, drawing her into the shelter of his body and sliding a hand under her chin to lift her face towards his so that she saw the darkness of his eyes. 'I'd like this to be your home too. I want both of us to live here. Yes,' he added gently as Micky's eyes widened at the realisation of just what he was saying, 'I *am* asking you to marry me, Midge.'

'Why?' Micky croaked foolishly. It was the only thing she could think of. Adam laughed softly.

'Because I love you, idiot child, that's why.'

The world swung around her, whirling crazily so that Adam's face was just a blur, and she shook her head savagely to clear her thoughts. She wanted to see his beloved face in this, the most wonderful moment of her life, see those beautiful eyes warm with the love he had declared, and watch them light up when she gave him her answer.

'I know I said I'd wait,' she heard Adam say. 'I tried to take things slowly, but—damn it, Midge! I can't wait any longer. I love you. I want you here, in my home, in my bed!'

Those last three words had the effect of a cold wind driving the mist from Micky's mind. She would say yes—how could she say anything else? But first she had to tell him.

'Adam.' Her voice was just a thread of sound. 'About Zac.'

'What about him?' Adam growled, angered by the way she had brought the other man's name into such a private moment. 'He's nothing to us any more and that's just the way I want it. After the way he talked about you that night in his flat he was lucky to escape with his life. I——'

Adam got no further. Her face white with shock, Micky cut in on him sharply, 'What night? When did you go to Zac's flat?'

'January. It was the obvious place to start looking for you. How the hell do you think I found out about that bedsitter of yours?'

'You talked to Zac?' Micky's voice was out of control, sliding up and down in the most peculiar way. 'What did he tell you?'

Did she have to ask? She could just imagine what sort of exaggerated version of their relationship Zac might have given, embroidering sordid details wildly.

'Tell me?' Adam echoed with blank incomprehension, then with shocking unexpectedness his expression softened into a sympathetic smile. 'Oh Midge, is that what's worrying you? Do you think I'd believe his pathetic lies when every instinct I possess tells me the opposite?'

'*What* did he say?' Micky persisted doggedly though her heart cried out at the self-imposed torture. 'I have to know!'

A dark frown clouded Adam's face at the memory. 'I'll spare you his exact words,' he said, his voice clipped and cold, 'but he led me to understand that your relationship had been a failure in every way, and that sexually you and he were—non-starters.'

When she had expected exactly the opposite, it was like a blow in the face, stunning her. What possible reason could Zac have had for claiming they had never been lovers? But then that hateful denunciation sounded in her head like the death knell to all her hopes. Oh yes, she could understand now. The time she had spent with Zac had taught her that he was eaten up with jealousy of anyone who had more than he did, and after the confrontation in her parents' house that jealousy had centred round Adam himself. She could just imagine how Zac would have felt when Adam turned up, looking for her. He would never imagine that any man could be put off by the thought that the woman he wanted had had other lovers, so when Adam came looking for her—and for Zac there could only be one reason for that—what better way to hit out at Adam than by implying that the girl he sought was completely frigid?

All this time Adam had been under the illusion that she was still a virgin. He had courted her, proposed to her in that belief—and it was all a lie! He said he loved her, but was his love strong enough to overcome his disillusionment when he discovered the truth? And how could she ever have dreamed of accepting his proposal knowing all the time that she had only second-best to give him? She loved him too much to sell him short like that.

With a wrench that tore at her heart as well as her body Micky pulled herself free from Adam's arms, desperately twisting away to put some distance between them so that he wouldn't see the pain and despair that burned in her eyes.

'No!' she cried harshly. 'No! No! No! I won't marry you—I don't want to marry you.' Her heart tore in half at the lie, but it had to be said. Better to hurt him—and herself—like this than to have him reject her when he knew the truth.

Something died in Adam's face as if a light had suddenly gone out, leaving the intangible barrier of total darkness between them.

'You can't mean that,' he said shakily.

'I do!' Micky muttered, then, as he shook his head,

she repeated more forcefully, 'I bloody well do! I don't want to marry you!' Her voice rose to a shout on the last words.

'Why the hell not?' Adam shouted back. 'You've given me every indication that you feel something for me—or was that all a lie?'

That nearly destroyed her. Dropping her eyes so that she wouldn't have to see the pain and anger blazing in his face, she murmured brokenly, 'No, it wasn't a lie. But I still won't marry you.'

'At least tell me why.'

Adam's sudden gentleness was more than she could bear. 'I've told you why! I *don't want you*!' she flung at him, using anger to hide the agony that ripped through her.

'I don't believe you.' Adam's voice was cold and hard as a steel blade and every bit as hurtful. 'If you said you didn't love me I might accept that—I'd have to—but you'll never get me to believe that you don't want me. You come alive when I touch you. If I were to kiss you now you'd feel it; we'd both feel it. Your body wants me, Midge. We were made for each other.'

He took a step towards her and Micky's legs threatened to buckle beneath her. If he touched her there was no way she would be able to resist him. There had to be some way to stop this once and for all! From somewhere in the recesses of her mind an answer came and she knew it was the only one, though her heart quailed at the consequences for herself if she took it. She would have to be utterly convincing—and Adam had said she wasn't a very good actress!

'You've got it wrong, Adam,' she heard the brittle, cruel voice that wasn't her own say clearly. 'I'm afraid I've been leading you on a bit, giving you the response you wanted because I do—care—for you. Zac was right, you know, I don't go for all this physical passion. Personally, I think the whole sex business is distinctly over-rated.'

In the appalling silence that followed the most hateful words she had ever spoken Micky raised her eyes fearfully to look at Adam and couldn't find him in the man who stood before her. Every trace of life had been wiped from the face of the man she loved; only his eyes were not dead but burning with a savage intensity of anger and disgust. She'd done it, Micky thought drearily. For better or worse she had made absolutely certain that he would never want to marry her now.

Slowly and defeatedly Adam bent his head, staring down at his hands that were clenched so tightly it seemed the bones might break through the tautly stretched skin. The movement caused a lock of hair to fall over his forehead and, unable to drag her eyes away from that chestnut brightness, Micky recalled on a pang of tenderness and longing how it had felt to tangle her fingers in that thick softness—but never again. If only—she dragged her mind away from that hopeless train of thought. There was *no* if only. She had been faced with a choice that was no choice. To tell him that Zac had been her lover or to pretend she didn't love him, either way led to the rejection she had read in Adam's eyes only seconds before. What was left of her heart shrivelled and died at the thought.

'Sex,' Adam muttered at last, his voice thick with loathing. Suddenly he flung his head up violently. 'You could at least have had the decency to call it making love!' he snarled savagely. 'To me it makes one hell of a difference!'

CHAPTER TWELVE

THE flowers were the first thing Micky saw when she walked into the living-room. After the ordeal of the journey home, she was ill-prepared for any further blows to her precarious self-control, but there was no hope that the beautiful bouquet could be from anyone but Adam. For so long he had held back on that special gift he knew would mean so much to her, and it was so like him to choose what he had believed would be a very important day for both of them to fill that particular gap in her life.

Micky had hung on to the remaining shreds of her pride for just as long as it took her to get inside the house, but now, well away from Adam's coldly contemptuous eyes, her legs gave way beneath her and she sank down on to the settee with the sharp cry of a wounded animal. For a long moment she stared down at the glorious mass of colour on her knee, her eyes blank and unfocused until she was jolted from her unhappy reverie by her mother's concerned voice. She blinked vaguely and caught sight of the square of card attached to the bouquet.

It was pure self-torture, she knew, but she had to know what Adam had written, what message he had sent her before the events of the afternoon had blasted them worlds apart. There was a masochistic sort of pleasure in simply seeing his handwriting, and Micky ran her fingertips along the line of script as if by that small gesture she could reach out and touch Adam too. But the words on the card danced in front of her eyes when she tried to read them. When at last her vision cleared and Adam's message stood out starkly on the white card Micky could only wish she had never seen them.

She had thought she was beyond feeling any more pain, thought her heart and mind too numbed by shock to feel anything, but Adam's message twisted the knife even deeper in the raw wound where her heart should be.

'The flowers say everything I feel', he had written and with a cry of anguish Micky gathered up the profusion of red roses with their promise of undying love, crushing them to her, heedless of the damage to the perfect blooms as she wept out her heartbreak and despair.

She had no recollection of when the roses had been taken from her, no idea when her mother had come to her side. She only knew that when the black tide of misery finally ebbed she was held close in the arms that had been there to comfort and soothe her when she was a child. And it was as she sobbed out the whole sorry story in response to her mother's gentle questioning that the final bitter irony came home to her like a blow to the head of someone already punch-drunk with pain.

At long last Adam had finally brought about the completion of his self-imposed task of reuniting Micky with her parents, because in her desolation she had confided in her mother in a way she hadn't done for years. She told her everything, withholding nothing, and though her mother's eyes saddened briefly at the truth about Zac, there was no hint of reproach or disapproval in her face when Micky's faltering voice finally ceased. It was the final healing of the estrangement there had been between them; never again would there be any restraint or concealment. They had found each other again—but at such a cost!

'Micky, love,' Mrs Dennison said at last, 'I want you to tell me something and I want an honest answer—this is too important for anything but the truth. Has Adam had other women—other lovers?' Then, as Micky nodded numbly, she went on earnestly, 'And do you mind?'

'No!' Micky cried vehemently. 'I *love* him! His past, the women in it, they're not important.'

'And don't you think he loves you enough to feel the same? Did you even give him a chance to tell you how he felt?'

'Oh, Mum,' Micky sighed. 'How could I ask him that? How could he not mind?'

'You don't.'

'But it's different for a . . .' Micky's voice failed her, her eyes suddenly huge in her pale face. It was as if Adam was standing behind her, speaking very close to her ear, so clearly did his voice sound in her head. Twice she had said just that to Adam and twice he had refuted her statement angrily. Amanda Dennison's heart lifted at the tiny spark of hope in her daughter's eyes.

'If he loves you, he loves you for what you are,' she said quietly. 'If his love is strong enough you'll both be able to put the past behind you—but you'll never know unless you tell him. It's wrong and cruel of you to judge him without giving him a chance to prove himself. You have to tell him the truth—and if Adam's half the man I think he is, he'll love you all the more for your courage and honesty.'

Honesty, Micky thought sadly. The quality she had so admired in Adam but had been lacking in herself. If she was honest now, was there any chance that Adam would listen? He had loved her, she had no doubt about that, but did he still love her or had she totally destroyed all that he felt for her? And if there was any feeling left was it *enough*?

Unconsciously Micky lifted her head, straightening her shoulders. Adam had called her a fighter, told her she had to fight for what she wanted, and he had asked her never to lose the spirit he saw in her. She would be letting *Adam* down if she didn't have one last try. But it was going to be so very hard because she hadn't the first idea where to begin.

* * *

The spade sliced through the soil as Micky pushed her foot down on it then twisted the blade to loosen the clod of earth. With a sigh of satisfaction she straightened up, stretching to ease her aching back, and surveyed the garden before her. She had three beds clear now, she was making progress. This was to be the herb garden—parsley, sage, rosemary and thyme, as it said in the song. Micky's eyes darkened in pain. Rosemary for remembrance. Would Adam ever look at her garden and remember?

A single tear trickled down her cheek and she brushed it away with a grubby hand, careless of the long streak of mud the movement left on her cheek. She had to keep busy or the pain would catch up with her. She couldn't give up now.

Give up! Micky repeated bitterly. There was nothing to give up on. Adam would never speak to her. If it hadn't been for the lights in the house she would never have known he had moved in, but he must know that she was here. Day after day she had worked in the overgrown garden and never once had she caught sight of the man she loved, unless she counted the dark, shadowy figure she sometimes glimpsed through a window.

'The garden's still yours!' Adam had flung at her as she got out of the car on that nightmare of a birthday, and so when she had determined to see him just once more, it had been the garden she had thought of as her only point of contact with him. But now she was forced to wonder if she was just fooling herself.

Micky shivered. It was bitterly cold and an icy wind stirred the skeletal trees against the horizon, warning of bleaker weather to come. As she turned to pick up the secateurs a dark shape at a bedroom window caught her eye.

So Adam was there again. How many days had she worked on doggedly as she did now, painfully aware of the silent observer at the window? It felt like a lifetime of them. He would never come out, never acknowledge her presence. He was a proud man and she had hurt him so terribly. If only she had the courage to walk up to the house and ring the bell—but she doubted that he would even answer it. Her jerky movements mirroring her troubled thoughts, Micky wielded the secateurs ruthlessly.

But tears blurred her eyes; her hand slipped awkwardly and she cried aloud in shock as the cutters sliced into her palm. Dropping the tool, she clutched the injured hand tightly, closing her eyes against the pain.

How long she stood like that she didn't know. It didn't seem long enough for anyone to have left the upstairs room, come downstairs and out into the garden, and she had heard no sound of footsteps, nothing to give her any warning. But when she opened her eyes again she thought that the shock must have affected her mind because Adam was standing before her, pale and gaunt in the grey light of the wintery afternoon.

'I—I cut my hand.' It was the only thing she could find to say, her brain seemed frozen, incapable of any coherent thought.

Unthinkingly Micky held the injured hand out towards Adam then watched unbelievingly as he took the grimy, work-roughened fingers in his own, his eyes fixed firmly on them, and lifted it slowly to his lips. In a dream she felt the warmth of his mouth on the long, shallow cut, on each separate mud-stained finger, and finally, lingeringly, on her palm. When Adam lifted his eyes to hers she saw the shadows under them, the lids heavy as if from lack of sleep, and the dull, lifeless look that drained all colour from his face. Even the bright glory of his hair seemed dimmed.

'I've missed you,' he said simply.

'Oh, Adam!' Micky choked and it was a cry of pain, of shock, of pleading all rolled into one.

Immediately something slid down over Adam's face,

something slight, indefinable, but it was like an intangible barrier, leaving him distant and withdrawn.

'You'd better come into the house and wash that cut,' he said curtly.

In the warmth of the kitchen Micky submitted passively to having her hand washed and the cut covered with a neat strip of sticking plaster, all without a word being spoken. Adam's touch was cool and impersonal, his expression remote in a way that was far more disturbing than the burning anger that had filled him when Micky had last seen him. It was as if he was frozen in ice, cut off from all feeling, and she didn't know how to reach him.

Speaking and moving like a robot programmed to play the polite host, Adam offered and made coffee. When he handed the cup to her, Micky unconsciously curled her fingers tightly round it as if its warmth might melt some of the ice that she now felt was enclosing her heart.

'Did you think any more about that idea of a florist's business?' Adam asked at last. His voice was flat and monotonous, no life, no emotion in the dead tones.

'Oh, I couldn't!' Micky protested. 'It wouldn't be right!' She could work in the garden, his gift of love, and be almost happy but it would destroy her to be in his home and yet completely cut off from him as she was now.

Adam's shoulders lifted in a dismissive shrug. 'It's up to you—but it seems a pity. This place is a family house—much too big for one person.' There was such a wealth of emptiness in the words that Micky felt her heart turn over at the sound.

'Have—have you done any more work on the house, any more decorating?' she asked diffidently, speaking to fill the silence.

'Some.' The single syllable was hardly encouraging.

'Do you like living here?'

In the same second that Micky registered the craziness of her sitting there making polite conversation when her whole future hung in the balance, Adam's head swung round to her and with a sensation like the stab of a red-hot knife she saw that some of the ice had melted and pain and loneliness burned in his eyes. But when he spoke his voice was that of a polite stranger.

'Not much,' he said in an obvious understatement. 'I'm thinking of selling it.'

'But why? You can't!—I mean—it's such a beautiful home.'

'It's a beautiful *house*,' Adam corrected coldly and the subtle alteration of that one word had the effect of throwing a stone into a pond, sending ripples of meaning reaching out far beyond what he had said.

'What do you mean?' Micky asked shakily.

'Godammit, Midge! You know!' Adam snarled.

Everything about him, the smouldering eyes, the deeply etched lines on his face, the tautness of every muscle in his body, warned her not to probe any deeper—but he had called her Midge, unconsciously, involuntarily perhaps, but it was one tiny sign that the ice had not completely reached his heart and it gave her a weak ray of hope.

'Tell me,' she said softly and winced as his fist slammed viciously into a cupboard door.

'You don't need telling!' he declared harshly. 'You know! You know what I planned—what I hoped for this house. I chose it for us—it was to be a home—*our* home! Without you it's nothing. If you're not here it's as cold and empty as that mausoleum of a place my father lived in before he died!'

Micky drew a long, shuddering breath of joy and fear. He had given her the opening she needed. The ice had split open, leaving a narrow crack through which she might just reach him.

'Adam,' she began tremulously then, exerting every

ounce of strength she possessed, she got a grip on her voice and continued more strongly. 'When your father cut himself off from Nina, how did you feel—about him?'

Doubt, confusion and blank incomprehension followed each other swiftly across Adam's face, but he answered her question frankly and with the honesty he had always given her.

'I thought he was a bloody fool—that he'd made an appalling mistake—and I tried to get him to see that. I begged him to reconsider, did everything I could to persuade him to make some move to end the feud. But at the same time I could see that he'd done what he had out of a misguided sort of love. He really believed that in opposing the marriage he was doing what was best for Nina, and didn't see his mistake until it was too late—and then he was too proud to admit it.'

The smile that curved Micky's lips would not be suppressed. He had said exactly what she had hoped he would. She saw that Adam was watching her warily, uncertainty clouding his eyes, and she continued hurriedly, 'And if someone else hurt another person in just that way, made that sort of mistake—out of a misguided sense of love,' she deliberately quoted his words back at him, 'would you help them to put it right?'

The swift change in Adam's expression took her breath away. All doubt and confusion vanished, to be replaced by an undisguised concern.

'Do you mean your parents? Midge, has something happened?'

'Oh, Adam, no!' Micky cut in sharply. 'Everything's fine—quite perfect. I wasn't talking about my parents!'

He had relaxed at her words but the last comment had him stiffening again. He took a step backwards and had to make a distinct effort to speak.

'Then who?'

Micky's throat felt constricted. It was as if all the

tangled emotions in her heart were forcing themselves upwards, choking her.

'I'm talking about me!' The words echoed round the silent room. '*I'm* the one who made the mistake—and hurt you so terribly by doing so. I did it out of love but it was all wrong—and now I want to put it right but I don't know how to, so I'm asking you to help me. Oh, Adam, please help me to make it up to you!'

The step Adam had taken away from her was reversed. He had moved one tiny fraction nearer, his hand lifting as if he would have touched her. Then he stilled the movement and let his hand stay half-raised, suspended between them like a lifeline, a promise of hope.

'Tell me,' he commanded softly.

Slowly and hesitantly, with a great many false starts and unfinished sentences, Micky forced the story out, and this time she held nothing back. She told him how, on the night she had left her parents' house, she had gone to Zac's flat; how she hadn't hesitated when he suggested they went to bed; how she had let him make love to her because it had been what they both wanted, because, at the time, she had thought that Zac really cared. It was an effort to keep the bitterness out of her voice when she recounted the disintegration of the relationship and the final break-up, but she had to be fair. Zac had hurt her, but he wasn't entirely the villain of the piece. He had conducted the affair according to his own selfish set of rules, never promising her any more than he actually gave, and she was the one who had deluded herself into believing that she could be happy with the little he offered.

When she finally stumbled to a halt, Micky realised with a sense of shock that, slowly and imperceptibly, Adam had moved nearer until now he stood at her side, his body almost touching hers. The hazel eyes were intent on her face as he spoke.

'Just one question,' he said slowly. 'Did you love him?'

And that was the hardest question of all. The answer burned in her throat. It would be so much easier to take the coward's way out and say yes, she had loved Zac—but Adam deserved much more than such half-truths.

'I thought I did but I was deceiving myself. I didn't know what love was. You see, I'd nothing to compare it with until I loved you.' She broke off in confusion, unnerved by the tenderness in his eyes.

'Poor Midge,' Adam murmured. 'Don't condemn yourself so harshly, sweetheart. Lots of girls go to bed with a man because they need to be held.'

At last his hand touched her, resting lightly on her hair, and after so many weeks of separation the fragile contact almost destroyed what was left of Micky's self-control.

'Can you forgive me?' she choked desperately.

'Forgive?' Adam repeated the word thoughtfully. 'I can forgive you for not telling me at first—I can understand that—but——' He paused, a frown darkening his face. 'I find it hard to accept that you didn't trust me enough—that you believed it mattered so much to me.'

'It doesn't?' Micky quavered, and with a sense of despair she saw the frown darken.

'Hell and damnation, Midge!' Adam exploded violently. 'What sort of bloody double standard do you think I work on? I'm no innocent—I've told you about Lauren—and there have been others, more than I'm proud of, but they're all behind me since I met you. If you love someone you take them as they are. No one's all black or pure white; we're all shades of grey, some darker than others. I don't expect you to throw my past in my face, so why the hell should I do it with you!'

The joy that was singing in her heart made Micky's head spin. It was a struggle to focus her eyes on Adam's face, to see the conviction that was written in every line. But she didn't have to see; she could hear what she needed in the burning intensity of his voice.

'I love you, Adam.' A whisper was all she could manage though if she had had the strength she would have shouted it aloud, wanting the world to hear.

'Oh, Midge!' It was a groan of happiness. 'My crazy, impossible Midge. I love you too, and *nothing* matters but that.'

The next moment she was in his arms, crushed up against his chest, hearing the pounding of his heart beneath her cheek and feeling her own pulse start to race in response. With a soft, wordless cry of joy she flung her arms around his neck, lifting her face for his kiss. Adam's mouth was hard on hers, bruising her lips with the strength of his passion, but Micky welcomed his lack of gentleness because it told her in a way that no words could ever express that the love and need and longing that flamed in her heart burned every bit as strongly in Adam's.

It was some time before either of them was calm enough to speak, but at last Micky heard Adam's voice whisper huskily in her ear, 'You'd better decide exactly what you want your wedding bouquet to say. I know November isn't the best time for flowers, but I have no intention of waiting till spring. I've spent too much time alone in this house already. I want you here with me every day and,' the hazel eyes darkened perceptibly, 'every night.'

Secure in the warmth of his love, Micky smiled her response.

'I believe holly means ecstasy,' she said mischievously, but then a shadow crossed her face. 'But Adam, I won't have anything special to give you! It won't be the first time.'

'Midge, stop it,' Adam reproved gently. 'Can't you see it will be the first time *for us* and that's all that's important to me?' Seeing the doubt that still clouded her face he drew her towards him again, pressing warm, enticing kisses on her face and throat, his hands moving over her body, caressing, arousing, promising joys she had never known.

'Let me show you, Midge,' he whispered against her lips. 'Let me help you put the past behind you once and for all and show you how wonderful the future—our future—will be.'

Wordlessly she let him lead her upstairs and lay her on his bed, soothing her tension with soft words and even softer kisses. He undressed her gently, caressing her as he did so, taking time to arouse her, give her pleasure, waiting in spite of the intensity of his own need until she was adrift on a sea of feeling and moaning his name aloud, no room for doubt in her mind, aware only of the longing that overwhelmed her.

But it was only at the exquisite peak of delight that Micky knew the whole truth of what had been missing before. In the white-hot moment of ecstasy every last uncertainty was burned away as she cried Adam's name aloud in joy that he had been right. She did have something invaluable to give him; she had her heart and all the love that was in it, a love given freely and unreservedly for the first and only time in her life. Nothing that had happened could take that away from her, just as nothing could ever tarnish the fact that Adam was the first man ever to teach her what making *love* really meant.